DEL...
FOS...

STORK
ALERT

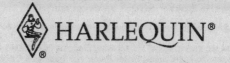

HARLEQUIN®

TORONTO • NEW YORK • LONDON
AMSTERDAM • PARIS • SYDNEY • HAMBURG
STOCKHOLM • ATHENS • TOKYO • MILAN • MADRID
PRAGUE • WARSAW • BUDAPEST • AUCKLAND

To Minette. This one's for you.

ISBN-13: 978-0-373-69275-0
ISBN-10:   0-373-69275-7

STORK ALERT

Copyright © 2007 by Delores Fossen

This is a work of fiction. Names, characters, places and incidents are either the product of the author's imagination or are used fictitiously, and any resemblance to actual persons, living or dead, business establishments, events or locales is entirely coincidental.

This edition published by arrangement with Harlequin Books S.A.

® and TM are trademarks of the publisher. Trademarks indicated with ® are registered in the United States Patent and Trademark Office, the Canadian Trade Marks Office and in other countries.

www.eHarlequin.com

Printed in U.S.A.

ABOUT THE AUTHOR

Imagine a family tree that includes Texas cowboys, Choctaw and Cherokee Indians, a Louisiana pirate and a Scottish rebel who battled side by side with William Wallace. With ancestors like that, it's easy to understand why Texas author and former air force captain Delores Fossen feels as if she was genetically predisposed to writing romances. Along the way to fulfilling her DNA destiny, Delores married an air force top gun who just happens to be of Viking descent. With all those romantic bases covered, she doesn't have to look too far for inspiration.

Books by Delores Fossen

HARLEQUIN INTRIGUE

*Five-Alarm Babies

Don't miss any of our special offers. Write to us at the following address for information on our newest releases.

Harlequin Reader Service
U.S.: 3010 Walden Ave., P.O. Box 1325, Buffalo, NY 14269
Canadian: P.O. Box 609, Fort Erie, Ont. L2A 5X3

CAST OF CHARACTERS

Kelly Manning—She's shocked to learn that someone switched her newborn son with another child. Kelly's investigation leads her to successful rancher Nick Lattimer, who's been raising her child.

Nick Lattimer—Joining forces with Kelly Manning was the last thing he expected. Can he keep Kelly and the babies safe?

Joseph—The son Kelly has raised since birth. Even though they don't share the same DNA, he's her child.

William—The baby Nick loves as his own. He's not willing to give up William to Kelly, even if she is his biological mother.

Eric Lattimer—Nick's ruthless brother who'll do anything, including commit murder, to make sure he doesn't have to share his inheritance with Nick's heirs.

Cooper Morris—The head of security at Nick's ranch.

Todd Burgess—A Justice Department agent who's trying to gather enough evidence to have Eric arrested.

Denny Russell—Kelly's P.I. friend who Nick immediately distrusts. Denny is keeping some dark secrets about his past.

Paula Barker—She's on the Justice Department task force that's trying to stop Eric, but does she have her own agenda?

Rosalinda McMillan—Eric's former secretary who claims she'll do anything to bring Eric to justice.

Collena Drake—The troubled, former cop who now devotes her life to finding out what happened in the Brighton Birthing Center where the babies were switched.

Chapter One

Bexar County, Texas

Kelly Manning checked to make sure no one was following her. No one was. She was alone in the dimly lit hallway.

So far, so good.

Too bad her pounding heart and racing breath didn't quite grasp that she was close to succeeding. A minute, maybe less, and she'd have what she needed and would be away from Nick Lattimer's ranch.

Of course, this could be just the beginning. Not exactly a comforting thought, but she would cross that bridge *if* she came to it. However, it was impossible to push aside the thought that the next few minutes could change her life forever.

She eased open the door to the nursery and ducked inside. The nanny was in the kitchen indulging in a late-night snack, so other than the baby, the suite would be empty. Timing was indeed everything. If any of the half-dozen or so "security guards" and household staff caught her, they would no doubt alert their boss.

Definitely not good.

Kelly hurried across the room to the crib. The baby was there. Sleeping. He was tucked beneath a blue satin-rimmed blanket. All she could see of him was the mop of blondish-brown hair, but with just that bit of visual info, she had to fight to hold on to her breath. Now wasn't the time to let her emotions get in the way of what she had to do.

With her hands trembling, she reached for the small vial she'd hidden in her bra. But reaching for it was as far as she got.

"Mind telling me what you're doing here?" she heard someone ask.

The sound shot through her entire body, and Kelly gasped. She didn't recognize the voice, but she had no doubt that it belonged to Nick Lattimer, the lord of the massive Texas ranch she was trespassing on. And he was the last person on earth she wanted to come face-to-face with tonight.

Heaven help her.

Dreading what she would see, Kelly angled her eyes in the direction of his voice. He was in the shadows, his shoulder resting against the doorjamb of the adjoining room. His head was slightly tilted to the side. Studying her. He wore a tux and a formidable take-no-prisoners expression.

"I was looking for the ladies' room," she managed to say. She'd practiced it enough that thankfully her voice didn't crack.

He pushed away from the doorjamb, a slick effortless move, and he started toward her. A pair of delicate angel night-lights illuminated his way. Ironic, since there was nothing angelic or delicate about him.

His midnight-black hair fell long and fashionably untamed against his neck. Dark, brooding eyes. Chiseled jaw. High cheekbones that hinted of Native American blood. He was handsome by anyone's standards.

Including hers, much to her disgust.

But his looks didn't make him less dangerous. From all accounts, he was an ends-justifies-the-means sort of man. *Any means.*

"The caterer and party staff were instructed to use the downstairs facilities," he informed her.

Kelly nodded. "I'm sorry, sir. I didn't know that." She turned to walk away.

Nick Lattimer shifted to the side and blocked her exit. He didn't stop there. He blocked her a second time when she tried to go around him. Then he circled her. Slowly. Like a hungry jungle cat stalking his prey.

Outside the window, lightning stabbed across the sky, quickly followed by thunder. The November storm only added to the menacing energy simmering around him.

"I wasn't joking about having to go to the ladies' room." Kelly tried to keep her tone light. She failed. Her heart was beating so hard and fast that she thought her ribs might crack.

He was behind her when she heard the whisper-soft sound. She might not have even known what it was. But she was a cop's widow.

It was a gun.

Oh, mercy.

It'd been a serious mistake coming here, but it was too late to turn back.

She got a good look at the weapon as he finished circling her and came to a standstill directly in front of her. Yes, it was definitely a gun. An expensive, high-powered Glock. Not an amateur's weapon of choice. It was too much to hope that he didn't know how to use it.

Her stomach tightened into a cold, hard knot.

Kelly forced herself not to panic. The stakes were too high for her to lose it. "Listen, I've obviously upset you by being here. It won't happen again."

"I don't doubt that. Only a handful of people have ever managed to upset me more than once." His narrowed gaze slid over her. "Who sent you?"

She'd anticipated a lot of questions. But not that one. Kelly shook her head. "What do you mean?"

"I mean… Who. Sent. You?"

Okay. It was clear from his sarcastic tone that he had his own issues and wouldn't let her just walk out. It was time to show a little backbone.

She hiked up her chin. "I understood what you said, but I thought the answer was obvious. I work for the caterer you hired for your dinner party." She pointed to her clothes. "You didn't think I was wearing this tacky polyester uniform to make a fashion statement, did you?"

"No. But it did occur to me that you were wearing it so you could gain access to my home. And to this particular room."

Without taking his lethal gaze off her, he reached out, snagged her by the shoulder and pushed her against the wall. Her right cheek landed next to a cheery cherub mural.

Other than a startled sound of protest, Kelly didn't have time to react before his left hand was on her. Moving across her back. To her sides. And her stomach. She battled with her instincts to fight back. But this wasn't a fight she could win. Not with his size and that Glock. Maybe once he realized she wasn't armed, he'd back off. Of course, he might find the vial. Even so, he likely wouldn't know what it was.

"So, is this how you treat your hired help?" Kelly snarled.

"It is when I find them in places they shouldn't be."

That searching hand went lower, to the stretchy waist of her dark-blue skirt. And even lower. He slid his palm along the outside of her legs. Then, the inside.

All the way up.

When his fingers made it to the lower front of her panties, Kelly grabbed his wrist and clamped onto his hand. Too bad she hadn't opted to wear her sturdy cotton underwear. Or her big-girl panties, as her grandmother used to call them. Instead, she had a little swatch of silk and lace that allowed her to feel every inch of his touch.

A touch she didn't want to feel.

She glared at him over her shoulder. "This isn't necessary."

"Oh, but it is," he countered.

Kelly had stopped his search in her panty region. Not the best idea she had ever had. Maybe it was her grip on his wrist, or maybe he was just a jerk—either way, he kept his hand there.

"Look, if this is your idea of foreplay—"

"It isn't." He threw off her grip and resumed his search. "Trust me, if it were foreplay, at least one of us would be enjoying it."

Apparently finished with the zinging smart-aleck comebacks and the search of her midsection, he caught on to her shoulder and whirled her around to face him. Kelly had to look up to meet him eye to eye. She was five-six, and he had a good seven inches on her. Plus, there was the weight difference. He outsized her by sixty pounds or more.

All muscle, no doubt.

He didn't look like the excessive-body-fat type. His size and strength would be a definite liability if she had to fight her way out of there.

Unfortunately, she might not have a choice about that.

"Were you trying to kidnap the baby?" Lattimer demanded.

That didn't do much to ease the knot in her stomach. Whatever she'd been expecting him to say, that wasn't it. "No! Absolutely not."

"Good. Because you would have failed." He tucked his gun inside a holster hidden beneath his jacket, reached over and threw back the blanket.

Stunned with his abrupt movement and with the fact that the baby didn't react to that movement, Kelly glanced in the crib. She didn't need the overhead light to realize it wasn't a baby but a doll.

A doll!

All of this had been for nothing.

"Listen carefully," Lattimer continued, speaking through nearly clenched teeth. He also got right in her face. "I don't tolerate thieves, even when they pose as polyester-wearing employees. I'm especially not fond of money-hungry opportunists like you who try to come in here and kidnap a child. No repeats of what happened to the Lindbergh baby. Understand?"

Somehow, Kelly managed to find enough breath to speak. "I'm not a kidnapper." This time, all the rehearsal in the world couldn't have stopped her voice from trembling. "I was just looking for the bathroom."

That repeated denial obviously didn't please him. His eyes, those dark dangerous gray eyes, narrowed to slits. He grabbed a fistful of her blouse, and without taking his gaze from hers, he reached inside. To her bra. It only took him a second before he retrieved the thin plastic vial.

Judas Priest. He must have seen her reach for it earlier.

"Did you plan to drug the baby?" he asked.

Lattimer didn't give her a chance to flat-out deny it. He opened it and extracted the swab that was enclosed in a clear plastic vial. He brought it to his nose. And sniffed it. Kelly knew for a fact there was nothing to smell because the swab was sterile.

"It's a lab test kit," she volunteered.

She took a deep breath and prayed he'd buy the lie she was about to tell him—especially since he obviously hadn't believed anything else she'd had to say. "My doctor thought I might have strep." Kelly purposely coughed on him and didn't cover her mouth, hoping it would spur him to let her leave. "I'm supposed to swab my throat and drop it off at his office."

He stared at it. A moment. Before he cursed under his breath. "It's not for strep. It's for a DNA test."

Nick Lattimer groaned, a feral sound rumbling deep from within his chest, and he launched the vial into the massive fireplace on the other side of the room. The plastic shattered when it hit the stone-lined hearth. "Who the hell sent you here?"

She barely got out a denying shake of her head before Lattimer latched on to her again. He put her back against the wall. Not nicely, either. He meant business.

"My ward, William, doesn't need another DNA test," he insisted. "Let me spell this out for you." He flicked on the overhead light and shoved his hands against the wall, imprisoning her. He leaned in, so close that she could see the swirls of gray and flecks of steel blue in his eyes. "William is not my biological child, and I have no plans to adopt him."

Kelly had suspected the first part.

She'd prayed for the second part to be true.

"William's *really* not your son?" she asked, desperate for him to confirm it.

"No." Lattimer mumbled something else under his breath. "I thought maybe once…but that doesn't matter. Not now. His mother is dead. He has no one else but me to raise him."

So, there it was. All laid out for her. The only thing missing was the proverbial silver platter.

"But I think William does have someone else to raise him," she whispered.

Something flickered in those icy blue-gray eyes. Surprise, maybe. Maybe something more. "Care to explain what you mean by that?"

Kelly nodded. "His mother's not dead." And because it was necessary, Kelly paused to clear her throat. "William is my son."

Chapter Two

William is my son.

Right.

Nick didn't know whether to laugh or curse some more. This woman was obviously delusional. Or maybe the person who'd hired her had brainwashed her into believing that she was indeed William's mother so that she would do whatever had been asked of her.

Now, the question was—what had been asked of her?

Who had done the asking?

And how far was she willing to go to get it done?

Nick looked her right in the eyes. "Let's try this again." He held up his index finger. "Who are you?" Another finger lifted. "Who hired you?" He put up a third finger. "And explain to me why the hell I should just let you walk out of here alive."

The threat garnered her complete attention. It also

seemed to rile her a bit. Nick was almost positive he saw a flash of anger rifle through her jade-colored eyes.

She reached out and pushed down one of his fingers. "I'm Kelly Manning." She pushed down another one. "I work for no one. Well, not on a regular basis anyway. I'm a freelance photographer in San Antonio." She wasn't so gentle when lowering his third finger. "And the reason I plan to walk out of here alive is because I've done nothing that warrants you trying to kill me."

"That's debatable."

Kelly Manning. Nick silently repeated her name several times to see if it rang any bells.

It didn't.

He was about to add another round of questions, but the door opened. It was Cooper Morris, the head of security for the ranch. A hulking man with a shiny shaved head and a body the size of a Sumo wrestler, Cooper took up most of the doorway. As if that wouldn't be intimidating enough to his visitor, he had his weapon drawn and ready to fire.

"Are you all right, sir?" Cooper asked.

Nick debated how much he should tell him and decided to keep things vague for a while. Later, he'd find out why it'd taken Cooper so long to respond to what could have been a dangerous breach of security.

"Ms. Manning and I were just chatting. *Ms. Kelly Manning*. It's possible that she's missed a dose of medication or something." That earned him a scowl from her. "Or perhaps the caterer is simply one of her many employers. Do a preliminary background check on her immediately. We'll be waiting here for your report."

Cooper glanced at her with his dark suspicious eyes before his attention came back to Nick. "Yes, sir." As Nick knew he would do, Cooper gave an efficient nod and disappeared, closing the door behind him.

If the threat of a background check bothered her, it didn't show. She certainly didn't cower in fear. She got to her feet and caught on to his arm.

"I want to see William," she insisted. *"Please."*

Even with the added *please,* he didn't have to debate this particular issue. "Under no circumstance will I let you anywhere near him."

Her grip tightened on his arm. "But I have to know if he looks like me. I have to know the truth."

"The truth? And just what might that be? That you have some insane fantasy that he's your son? Well, he's not. Understand? *He's not.*" He slung off her grip. "His mother was Meredith Beirce, my late friend, and she died the very evening she gave birth to him."

"Yes, I know. On October eighth, at the Brighton Birthing Center just outside of San Antonio," she said without hesitation.

Nick didn't hesitate, either. "Anyone could have learned that from public records."

"That's not how I knew," she insisted. "I met Meredith several times. We used the same obstetrician, and we went into labor on the same day. And, yes, I also know that she died at nine twenty-three p.m. of complications from a respiratory infection."

Nick shrugged. "If you think knowing that information will impress me, you're dead wrong."

"It wasn't meant to impress you."

Without warning, she caught on to the waist of her skirt and shoved it down to expose her stomach.

Her bare stomach.

And then she lowered it even more. He could see the top of her ruby-colored panties, the ones he'd felt when he searched her.

"See that?" she asked. "It's a C-section scar. I gave birth to a son the morning of October eighth at the Brighton Birthing Center."

Nick glanced at the scar in question. He'd never seen a C-section incision but didn't doubt that was one. "It proves nothing other than you've had a child. A child. It doesn't mean that child was William."

She groaned and fixed her skirt. He almost thanked her for covering herself. For reasons he didn't want to explore, his body reacted to hers in the most basic male way it could react. It was purely a lust thing. No doubt about it. But he didn't even want lust playing into this.

He wanted no connection whatsoever with this woman.

She plowed both hands through the sides of her short choppy blond hair and took several harsh breaths. "If I weren't on the receiving end of these thug tactics, it might please me to know that you're going to such great lengths to take care of William. You're making sure he isn't kidnapped by someone out to earn a quick buck. But how about you just hear me out before you start tossing around any more accusations?"

He gestured for her to go ahead. But hopefully the scowl on his face would let her know that her explanation meant nothing.

"Thirteen months ago, on October eighth, I had a son, and four days later, I left the birthing center with the child I thought was mine." Her bottom lip started to tremble, and tears glistened in her eyes. She quickly blinked them back. "This isn't easy for me. I love my son, Joseph, more than life itself. And he's all I have."

He nodded. Nick could understand that. He felt the same way about William.

She returned his nod. "I'm not asking for sympathy, even though heaven knows I might need some before this over. Still, I don't expect I'll get it from you." Rather than look at him, she stared at the mural behind him. "About a week ago, I got a visit from a woman named Collena Drake. She's been going through files and records from an illegal adoption ring that the San

Antonio police uncovered and stopped. Collena found a memo indicating that someone paid for two babies to be swapped at Brighton."

Nick shrugged. "Why would anyone pay for something like that?"

She paused. Seemingly to steady her breath. But that pause didn't do much to steady him.

Hell.

Nick didn't like where she seemed to be going with this, but he reminded himself that she was almost certainly a liar.

"I have no idea why someone would want to switch babies, but I can't dismiss that it happened. In fact, I have some proof that it did."

"What proof?" he fired at her, feeling more and more uncomfortable with this whole conversation.

"My late husband and I had the same blood type," she continued. She moistened her lips. "Joseph doesn't. And before you ask—no, I didn't cheat on my husband. In fact, he's the only man I've ever had sex with."

Nick had conditioned himself not to respond instinctively to anything, but this was testing the limits of his training. "And why would you think any of this would be of the slightest interest to me?"

Kelly Manning looked him straight in the eye. "Because it's my guess that William and Joseph were the babies who were switched."

After getting past the initial punch of shock, he

gave that some thought, looking for a flaw in her theory, and he found one immediately. "There were probably dozens of babies born on that day."

"Five boys," she quickly furnished. "I've checked all of them. Either through blood type or ethnicity, I was able to rule them out. Except for William. He's the last name on my list."

It was a good attempt to get him to believe her. Very good. But it didn't work. "If you suspected a baby switch, why didn't you just go to the police?"

She flinched. Yet more of the proof that Nick was looking for. Well, maybe it was proof. If so, now he had to wonder why she was doing it. Money, maybe? Or maybe she really did work for his brother.

"Put yourself in my place," Kelly Manning explained. "My husband, a police officer, was shot and killed when I was barely two weeks pregnant, and then I learned the child—our child—wasn't really ours after all. I was afraid the police or social services would take Joseph from me until they could investigate what happened. So, I decided to try to get to the truth on my own."

There was more to it. He'd bet his life on it, but Nick didn't push it because frankly it didn't matter. "If you carry this illogical speculation out to its equally illogical conclusion, then you're saying that this baby, Joseph, is really Meredith's biological son?"

"I think so, yes." Her gaze snapped to his. "But

she's dead so she can't take him away from me. And I checked—she has no living relatives. *None.* That's why you agreed to raise William, right?"

Nick didn't bother to answer that. It wasn't any of this woman's business that he'd felt an obligation to his former lover.

Kelly stared at him. "You don't believe a word I've said, do you?"

"You're a very perceptive woman. Which makes me wonder why you came here with this outlandish story in the first place. Did my brother, Eric, put you up to it?"

"No!" She repeated it, groaned and slapped her hand against the wall. "I don't even know your brother. And I didn't come here to kidnap a baby or do anything else that would harm him." The outburst was short-lived, but it seemed to drain her. Her chin lowered a notch, and she turned away from him. "I just want to know the truth, all right? I want to know, for certain if William is my son."

He heard her breath shudder again. He heard the pain. And he saw her wipe the tear from her cheek. She was either a very good actress, or else...

Nick put a chokehold on that particular thought. He didn't intend to give her any concessions until he had that background check from Cooper.

"All I'm asking for is a DNA test," she said almost in a whisper. "A simple saliva swab."

"That's not going to happen. Not until I know more about you. And even then…"

Her sigh was long and weary. "Then just listen and do the math yourself. My late husband and I are both O negative. That means our child must be type O, as well. Notice the operative word there. *Must*." She paused a moment. "Joseph is type B. B negative, to be exact." Another pause. "So, this is more than a wild guess, but William has type O blood, doesn't he?"

He did.

So did millions of people.

However, that wasn't what sent Nick's mind racing and his heart pounding. It was the added remark his visitor had tossed out there. The other child's blood type.

B Negative.

Nick's own rare blood type.

His mind continued to race until the possibilities crashed down on him like an avalanche.

If Meredith had lied to him. If his first instincts had been right after all. If she had indeed been pregnant with his child when she walked out and left him.

Then, maybe he had a son.

If that were true, then he would certainly come face-to-face with his worst nightmare.

Because any son of his would automatically be a target for murder.

Chapter Three

"Did you hear what I said?" Kelly asked.

Somewhere in the middle of her crucial explanation about blood types, Nick Lattimer had taken a mental hike. Sweet heaven, he was either totally heartless, or he didn't have a clue what this was doing to her.

"I heard you." He slid his hands into the pockets of his perfectly tailored tux and strolled to one of the bay windows that flanked the fireplace.

"Then you no doubt understood that Joseph can't be my biological son."

He made a sound that could have meant anything, and continued to stare out the window.

Because she had no choice, Kelly kept trying. "That's why I need to do the DNA test on William."

She felt the tears threaten again and forced them back. She wouldn't cry. Not in front of him, anyway. Showing such weakness might make him go for her jugular, and right now she felt way too exposed.

"There have already been DNA tests done on William," he let her know.

"Yes, but those were to prove that he isn't *your* son. We need to do another one. A maternity study, they call it. So we can compare William's DNA to mine."

"And then what?" he fired back.

Kelly fully understood the implications of that simple question, and she didn't like it any better than he apparently did. "I don't know. Honestly, I don't. But I can't just forget what I've learned. I can't walk away and pretend this never happened. Believe me, I've tried."

"I'll bet you have."

"So, we're back to the sarcasm." Kelly didn't let it deter her. "Look, I don't have all the answers, but this test is a start. We'll get the results and go from there." She waited a moment, hoping her voice would remain steady. "If there are any existing DNA samples for Meredith, I could have them compared to Joseph's."

"There are no samples. Meredith was cremated at her request and her ashes scattered on the grounds of her childhood home."

Well, that was that. Another roadblock. Or else another stonewall attempt. Either way, it was a very hard place for her to get past.

But not an impossible one.

"Then, what about the biological father?" Kelly

had to take a hard breath before she could continue. "Is there a chance he'd try to take Joseph if he finds out about him?"

She braced herself for whatever Nick Lattimer was about to tell her. It could easily be a bombshell that she wasn't ready to have dropped on her. But he didn't say a single word. He just kept his stiff back turned to her while he looked out the window.

Kelly groaned. "Look, this silent treatment is getting on my nerves. This might sound like a bad cliché, but I'm not even sure if I can handle the truth. Still, I have to know, all right? I can't go on wondering if I have a son that I've never even met."

He glanced at her over his shoulder. She thought she might have seen some sympathy in his eyes, a sliver of it anyway, but if so, he didn't get a chance to voice it. There was a knock at the door. One sharp rap.

"Come in, Cooper," Lattimer ordered, not even bothering to verify that's who was at the door.

However, it was indeed the bald-headed giant who'd made an appearance earlier. He gave her a considering glance. And a distrustful one. The feeling was mutual. Kelly didn't trust him either. Of course, that probably had something to do with the fact he worked for Nick Lattimer.

"I've got the preliminary background check," Cooper told his boss.

"Read it."

The bald guy gave her another glance. "Out loud, sir? With her in the room?"

"Read it," Lattimer insisted, the impatience straining his voice.

Those repeated two words and the stark edginess were apparently enough for the man to spring into action. "Her name is Kelly Baker Manning. I confirmed it with the photo on file at the Department of Motor Vehicles. Age twenty-eight. No criminal record. Self-employed as a photographer—she does mainly weddings and birthday parties. Widowed. Spouse was Louis Manning, vice detective, San Antonio PD. Killed in the line of duty. She has a thirteen-month-old son, Joseph Louis Manning. I also have her address and phone number."

All the information was correct. Kelly checked her watch. Less than ten minutes, it'd taken him to get her life story. Well, most of it anyway. In this case, the bare facts didn't really tell what she'd been through.

Or what she was no doubt facing.

"She didn't lie on her job application to the caterer," Cooper went on. "Not that I can tell anyway. I'll keep digging though."

No surprise there. By morning, she'd be an open book to them. Which wasn't necessarily a bad thing. Maybe then Lattimer would believe some of what she'd told him and allow the DNA test.

Of course, maybe he'd have her arrested for trespassing.

"She asked the nanny about the baby and the location of the nursery," Cooper explained further.

"I know," Lattimer informed him. "And the nanny purposely gave her false information and then alerted me as she'd been instructed to do."

That's how Lattimer had known she was there in the fake nursery. So much for her plan. She'd underestimated him right from the start.

Cooper aimed a scowl at her. "Should I call the authorities or escort her off the ranch?"

"No. I'll take care of the situation." There was an unspoken adios and get-lost at the end of Lattimer's remark, and Cooper obeyed without so much as batting an eyelash.

"Satisfied that I'm not some criminal?" she asked Lattimer the moment Cooper shut the door.

"No."

Mercy. It was like banging her head against a wall.

Just when Kelly thought that things couldn't possibly get any more frustrating, she felt the phone vibrate in her pocket.

"What's wrong?" he asked.

Only then did she realize that Nick Lattimer was looking at her. And not just looking, either. *Staring* at her. The way he'd done when they first laid eyes on each other.

"That'll be from my sitter." She took out the phone just long enough to glance at the text message to verify that's indeed who it was. "I told her to text me if Joseph woke up in the night. He did. He's not used to me being gone, and I didn't want him to be frightened."

He stayed quiet a moment. "Do you need to go to him?"

"Not really. He's not crying or anything, or she would have said. He should be all right."

A muscle flickered in his sleek jaw. "Still, there's no reason we have to work out all of this tonight. You should go home to him. I'll have someone drive you."

"That's not necessary. My car is already here. Besides, I don't want to be brushed off. I want to know—"

"I'll consider your request for another DNA test for William, and I'll inform you of my decision as soon as I've made one."

The abrupt about-face along with her tangled nerves nearly caused Kelly's legs to give way. "Why the change of heart?"

"Because you've caught my attention. Hopefully, you haven't caught anyone else's." He didn't add more regarding that ominous comment. "If I do consent to the test, I'd prefer to have a complete picture. Or as you so cleverly put—*a start.* That means you'll allow me to have your son's DNA tested, as well."

It made her ache to think of someone, some

stranger, out there who might have a legal claim on Joseph. However, she understood his request all too well, since she felt the same need to find out the truth about William. Blood wasn't necessarily thicker than water, but she couldn't deny the pull it had on her.

"Do you happen to know who Joseph's biological father is?" Kelly asked, dreading the answer, but knowing that she needed it.

The muscles went to work again in his jaw. "No."

She was either paranoid, or that was a lie. "Meredith and I talked a few times. She didn't mention him, other than to say he wasn't in the picture."

"She didn't talk about him to me, either," he insisted, his voice tight.

So, unless the father was dead, he was out there somewhere. But what Kelly had going for her was that he hadn't tried to claim William so far, and that meant he probably wouldn't try to claim Joseph, either.

She prayed.

And that was one of the reasons she hadn't wanted this baby switch in the hands of the police. Or the press. Newspapers tended to pick up that kind of story, and while she couldn't keep Joseph's biological father from seeing him, she truly hoped Meredith was right—that he wasn't in the picture.

This way, Kelly could proceed with her plan. First, verify that William was her son. Then petition the court for custody of both boys.

Well, she could after she got past one more obstacle.

"You said you had no plans to adopt William." She paused, and mentally wrestled with how she should say this. "Is that because you don't want children?"

Nick Lattimer turned, faced her. Behind him, the rain and the wind assaulted the window. There was even a dramatic slash of lightning across the night sky. He stood in the center of the glass. Calm. Except for one thing. His right hand had clenched into a fist.

"You honestly don't know about my brother?" he questioned.

Confused, she shook her head, not sure where this was leading. "I know you have one," she said. Kelly tried to recall her research notes. She'd read a mention or two of his brother, but that was it. She couldn't imagine what he had to do with any of this.

"Among other things, Eric is *possessive,*" he explained. He shoved his hands back into his pockets. "With things, not people. He inherited the bulk of the family estate, which, according to the terms of my mother's will, he doesn't have to share with me."

Oh. She got it. Kelly quickly filled in the blanks. "But Eric would have to share with your heirs?"

He nodded. "Except he wouldn't share. My brother is a violent, dangerous man."

That sank in quickly, too. Kelly flattened her hand over her chest and dropped back a step. "Are you saying he would hurt a child of yours?"

Nick Lattimer walked closer, his footsteps punctuated with a roll of thunder. "Not *hurt*. Eric would eliminate the child."

That sent her heart to her knees and stole her breath. "I'm sorry. So sorry. Now, I understand why you were concerned. You thought your brother sent me here to get the DNA sample."

"It wouldn't be the first time. But I thought that after three tests, one of which I let his personal physician perform, that Eric's fears would be put to rest."

It was a chilling revelation, but Kelly couldn't help but think this would fuel her case to get custody of her son. Nick Lattimer might even welcome having William away from his brother's paranoid watchful eye.

Kelly knew she would welcome it.

She didn't want her son associated with a would-be killer, and as long as William remained at the Lattimer ranch, he would be in danger. It was sickening to think of it. She wouldn't go through that again.

She couldn't.

She hadn't been able to save her husband, but she could certainly do something to save their child.

"May I see William?" Kelly had to clear her throat and repeat it so it would have sound.

Lattimer didn't respond. Seconds passed. Very slowly. And even though there were no overt signs of the debate he was having with himself, Kelly knew there was indeed a debate. But after what he'd just told her, she could understand why. Maybe he still didn't trust her. Maybe he thought she was working for his brother, Eric.

And maybe he simply realized that he could lose William to her.

After all, he'd raised William for thirteen months and no doubt loved him as she loved Joseph.

"A photo will do for now," Kelly added. "If you agree to the test, well, maybe then…"

He hitched a shoulder toward the doorway where she'd first spotted him. "Follow me."

She did, after Kelly got past the initial shock and after she got her legs to cooperate. Nick Lattimer had already given her a huge concession just by agreeing to think about doing the DNA test. She certainly hadn't really expected him to allow her to see William.

The adjoining room was just as lavishly decorated as the fake nursery. A sitting room of sorts. With another fireplace, a pair of oversize cushiony chairs, and a great view of the formal gardens. It'd be an ideal place to spend some quiet time with a child.

All along, since the moment she'd known she would be coming to the ranch, Kelly had tried not to think of how her biological son was being raised. Literally, in the lap of luxury. There was no way she could compete with this.

Yet, even that certainty wasn't enough to stop her

from getting the truth. Or from getting custody. Because she could give William something that Nick Lattimer couldn't. She could give him safety, away from Nick's brother.

He pressed something on the underside of the mantel, and the serene pastoral painting above it disappeared. It'd been a hologram on a thin screen. A very convincing one. Another room appeared.

A nursery.

A real one.

Without saying a word, he pressed more buttons beneath that mantel so that a camera zoomed in on the crib. No blue-satin-trimmed blanket this time. The child was covered with a very homey-looking quilt. A mobile of colorful butterflies dangled overhead.

Kelly had tried to prepare herself in case this moment ever came, but there was nothing that could have prepared her for this. William lay there, sleeping. And thanks to the high quality of the surveillance camera, she could see him clearly.

She pressed her fingertips to her mouth to muffle the sound that was trying to make its way past her throat. He was, well, precious for lack of a better word. A round angelic face. Golden-blond hair that tended to curl. His lips were pursed slightly. He seemed healthy. And perfectly content.

That didn't do a thing to lessen the guilt that was starting to roar through her.

The guilt went up a significant notch when she caught sight of Nick Lattimer's expression. Definitely not the face of a heartless, callous businessman.

It was the expression of a loving father.

And it cut her to the bone.

Because she could factor in many elements. The fact that Joseph's birth mother was dead. The fact that his biological father likely wouldn't challenge her for custody. But Kelly couldn't discount that Nick Lattimer loved this child as his own.

A child that was almost certainly hers.

That love for William was the ultimate obstacle that wouldn't be easy to overcome. But she would.

Somehow.

Kelly was resolute about that. But that didn't mean she was immune to that loving, fatherly look in Nick Lattimer's eyes.

"I should go," Kelly managed to say. Mercy. Now, she was *really* feeling guilty. "I need to get home to Joseph." She didn't wait for Lattimer's response. She headed out the way they'd come in.

He followed her. Of course. And he caught her arm just before she made it to the door. "I don't want you to say anything about this to anyone," he insisted. "Understand?"

"Of course." Probably because he didn't want Joseph's biological father or anyone else to get word of it before they could figure out what to do. And then there was the issue of Eric. She definitely didn't want his creepy brother thinking there was a competing heir.

She stood there a moment. Their gazes connected. Those gunmetal eyes no longer seemed as lethal as they had minutes earlier. Even though she figured it was temporary. Lattimer hadn't gotten his steely reputation by accident.

"Thank you," she told him. "I think."

The corner of his mouth lifted. Just slightly. And for only a split second. It wasn't an expression of amusement but more of irony.

Since the moment quickly became awkward, she fluttered her hand toward the door. "I'll just go."

And she did. She hurried out of there before he could stop her. Kelly raced down the back staircase and grabbed her purse and keys from the kitchen. Thankfully, everyone was busy with the preparation for serving dessert, so no one said anything to her as she walked out.

The late-autumn rain pelted her as she hurried out of the house and to her car. She made it all the way off the ranch before the tears came. With them came the doubts and the sickening feeling in the pit of her stomach. With all his money and contacts, would Nick Lattimer fight her for custody even if she proved that William was her son?

Those questions repeated in her head, and Kelly began to think of all the things Lattimer could do to prevent her from assuming custody. However, even with the tears, the violent storm and the painful question, she didn't miss the other car.

The black SUV appeared less than a minute after she drove through the massive wrought-iron gates that fronted Lattimer's property. The vehicle stayed steady behind her on the country road. A safe distance away so that most people might not have noticed.

She noticed.

And it sent a deathly chill over her.

God, what had she done?

Chapter Four

Nick took the turn on Old Cypress Road, noted the parked dark-green car with the heavily tinted windows and let the bit of information he'd just learned sink in. Well, as much as information like that could sink in. Now the question was—was it relevant to Kelly Manning's visit to the ranch?

"She was under psychiatric care at St. Mary's Hospital a little over a year and a half ago," Cooper added, his voice clear on the tiny speaker of Nick's cell phone. "For severe depression. She was treated and released after just two days, but she still sees a therapist a couple of times a month."

Nick moved those details around in his head, fitting them to the other facts he already had in place. "A year and a half ago. That was about the same time her husband was killed."

"Yes. About a week after."

"So, it's reasonable that she might need professional care to get through something that traumatic. Especially since she was only a few weeks pregnant."

"I suppose. But there's the fact that it took me too many layers to find anything about this particular hospital stay. Someone buried her file, sir. Trust me, that's not easy to do these days."

Nick had no doubts about that. Especially since he had the resources to dig through layer after layer of anything that a person might want to hide. However, a brief stay in the mental ward of a hospital didn't make Kelly Manning insane.

Nor did it exonerate her of anything.

She could still be a liar. An opportunist. Or a half dozen other unsavory things, including but not limited to Eric's employee.

On the other hand, if she truly was an innocent party in all of this, then God help her. She'd just wandered into a viper's nest.

And he was one of the very vipers that could end up getting her killed.

"Sir, I'm asking you to rethink this visit," Nick heard Cooper say. "You shouldn't go to see this woman alone."

But that was the only way this visit would happen. It was too dangerous otherwise.

"I'll be fine, Cooper. Besides, you have one of your men posted nearby." It wasn't a question. Nick had seen the security guard in the dark-green car and knew it was one of his vehicles and employees.

"I do. But he won't be inside."

"Nor do I want him there," Nick insisted, making sure he got his point across. He appreciated Cooper's concern, but this visit had to happen solo. The authoritative tone was a surefire way to make certain Cooper backed off.

Nick brought his car to a stop one block up from her house. He took his phone off the speaker function, got out of his car and, despite the crisp air from the cold front moving in, walked the rest of the way. Best not to announce to the world that he was there, by parking his car right in front of her house.

"Keep looking for more of Ms. Manning's *layers* and whatever turns out to be beneath them," Nick instructed Cooper. "If she's hiding anything, or if you find even a remote connection to Eric, I want to know immediately."

Nick ended the call and stopped in front of Kelly Manning's house. It was an odd little place. Though it was still on the fringes of the city, it was almost like a fairy-tale cottage with its charcoal-gray-slate-tiled roof, pristine ivory exterior, pale yellow shutters and cobblestone walkway. There were now empty flower beds beneath the pair of front bay windows, but he imagined that in the spring those beds would be bursting with color.

The only thing missing was a white picket fence.

However, the picture wasn't quite so pastoral to Nick. For one thing, the house was isolated on a huge lot choked with thick trees and shrubs. Securing it would be a nightmare. Yet it would have to be done.

And soon.

Nick checked his coat pocket to make sure William's DNA sample was there. It was. He also had two other sterile buccal swabs enclosed in their equally sterile containers. One was for Kelly Manning. The other for Joseph. Even now, nearly thirty-six hours after her visit, Nick was still debating if he should give William's DNA sample to her. A refusal might lessen the danger.

Maybe.

Or maybe it would just make her dig even harder to get to the truth.

Digging in this case wouldn't be a good thing. If her search alerted Eric's people, and it almost certainly would, then it'd be more than her life at stake. So, it was probably best to give her the sample and then monitor anyone who had access to the results. If worse came to worst, then he could always alter the tests to keep everyone safe.

Nick followed the cobblestone walk to the front porch. He paused a moment, to make sure he could pull off his famous iceman act, but the door opened before his pause had hardly started.

And there she was.

Kelly Manning was staring up at him through the clear glass storm door. "I'd just about decided that I'd have to make another visit to the ranch," she greeted. She wiped her paint-splattered hands on an equally paint-splattered rag.

The comment was friendly enough, but he heard the nerves simmering right there beneath the surface. The wait had obviously put her through hell. Little did she know it'd done the same to him.

"Did I come at a bad time, Ms. Manning?" he asked.

"Well, that's the polite thing to ask, but you and I both know there is no good time for this." She held open the storm door. "Oh, and drop the Ms. Manning part. Kelly will do."

"Nick," he reciprocated.

Without the door between them, Nick could see what she was wearing. Faded, well-worn jeans that rode low on her hips and a snug little stretchy top the color of a chili pepper. It outlined her breasts. Of course, her breasts were the last things that Nick wanted to notice. He was going to have to ignore the fact that she was attractive.

Damn attractive.

It was the lust factor. It had to be. Why his body began to hum and simmer when he was around this woman, he didn't know. He didn't want to know, either. Nick just wanted it to stop.

"Come in." She stepped aside so he could enter.

The place didn't smell like paint, even though she'd obviously been working on an oil portrait just a couple of yards away from the door. Instead, he caught a whiff of baby powder.

And her.

Something distinctly female. Somehow, it was that unique scent that cut through everything and made its way to his nose. Nick reminded his nose not to get any bad ideas to pass on to the rest of his body.

He forced his attention away from her and looked around the simply furnished room. It evidentially did double duty as a living area and studio. It was clean, uncluttered and efficient. A lot like the woman who owned it. What was missing was the baby, Joseph. But there were two rooms just off to his left. One of them was probably the nursery.

She motioned for him to take a seat on the perky floral sofa. "Why did you think the guards were necessary?" she immediately asked.

Nick blinked. "Guards?"

She pointed to the window. "The one up the street who followed me home the other night. Either he or his partner has been sitting out there the entire time. They've changed off shifts and cars, of course, probably so they wouldn't be so conspicuous. It didn't work."

This time he suppressed the blink. "The guards are just a precaution."

"You know, you do that a lot—avoid answering very direct questions." She dropped down into the chair across from him and tucked her feet beneath her. "If the guards are here to keep an eye on me, to see if I'm up to anything criminal, then they're wasting their time and your money."

"That's one of the reasons they're here," he admitted. "But I was also concerned about your safety."

"How admirable of you." And she didn't sound as if she meant it. "But my safety won't be an issue once I prove that William is my son. Both he and I will be safe then."

Nick wouldn't bet on that.

Since this visit was getting more uncomfortable in just about every way possible, he held up the test kit with William's DNA sample. It was clearly labeled to prevent a mix-up with the other kits.

She stared at it a moment before she tossed her paint rag on the lamp table and took it from him. "Is that what I think it is?"

"Yes." Nick didn't add more. He let her take the lead.

"Wow." She flexed her eyebrows. "I would have liked to have been a fly on the wall when you finally made the decision to go through with this."

"It would have been a very boring event to witness." The battle had all been within. He could say the same about the particular battle he was fighting now. All within. Well, except for that blink.

"No gnashing of teeth?" she asked.

He shrugged. "Maybe some. But I figured this was the fastest way to disprove your allegation."

"Ah, so you're back to thinking I'm a liar. Of course, 'disprove your allegation' sounds so much more civil, doesn't it?"

"I thought so," Nick said, playing along with her sarcasm. He extracted the blank, sterile kits, as well. "One is for you. The other is for Joseph."

She eyed the vials much as she'd eyed him at the ranch. As if they were deadly. In so many ways, they could be.

Kelly didn't waste any time. She opened one kit and wiped the swab on the inside of her cheek. She placed it back in the vial and used a pen from the drawer to label it. "I'll take a sample from Joseph as soon as he wakes up from his nap."

So, the baby was there at the house. Nick didn't know if that was good or bad. He'd prepared himself for either and knew no amount of mental preparation would help him for what he might face.

She carefully placed the test kits on the table. "I'm trying really hard not to be terrified of you, but I'm failing. You scare the heck out of me."

Her honesty had a way of breaking down his defenses. Not good. He couldn't allow that. "Terror isn't always a bad thing. My reputation—"

"I didn't mean your reputation as a ruthless, cutthroat businessman. I'm talking about Joseph." Kelly moistened her lips and took in a quick breath. "Despite my need to learn the truth about the swap, I'm sick with fear over the possibility of losing Joseph."

But that was all she said about what she was feeling. As far as she allowed the emotion to go. Another breath. Another moistening of her lips. Another flex of her eyebrows. And the display of emotions was over. She tucked them neatly away much as she did the stray blond lock of hair that she lifted off her cheek and slid behind her ear.

"So, what juicy things did the bald guy find out about me?" she asked.

Nick chose his answer carefully. "Cooper was thorough, as he always is."

"You did it again. You evaded the question."

She smiled. It was laced with nerves, but it still lit up her whole face. He felt another quick punch of lust. Fortunately for him, the smile faded as quickly as it'd come. Obviously, she too remembered there was little about their situation that warranted a smile.

"Let's see. If he was thorough, *as he always is,* then you know I was raised by my aunt because my parents died when I was a kid," she went on. "That wouldn't have necessarily reinforced the concerns you have about my potential criminal tendencies. But the two-day stay in the psych ward would have given you a few troubled moments."

Surprised by her stark honesty, Nick nodded. "A few."

She leaned forward a little. "I don't owe you this, but I'll tell you, anyway. It happened. I could provide you with a lengthy recount of why, when and where, but I'm sure you already know the *when* and *where* parts."

"And I guessed the *why*."

"Yes, I'll bet you did." She paused and glanced at the vials. "You appear to be a smart man, and I don't consider myself an idiot, so here goes. For one moment, assume that I'm not lying. That there was indeed a baby switch. What happens when we get the results from these tests?"

Nick was trying not to think of that nightmare.

"I'd prefer to wait for the results," he insisted. "I think once we have those, there won't be a decision to make. Because I don't believe there was a switch."

"But you've thought about it. A lot. I'm sure of that. So have I. If they confirm what I already know in my heart, I'll ask for custody of William." She snared his gaze. "But then, Joseph's father could do the same for him. If his father is anywhere around, that is. Or if he even wants custody."

That seemed like her attempt to get him to speculate or confess, but there was no way he could engage in that particular discussion. Thankfully, he didn't have to put her off. The two sounds happened almost simultaneously. Nick's phone rang, and the baby started to cry.

On a ragged sigh, she grabbed all three of the test kits and got out the chair. "I'll be back." And she disappeared into one of the other rooms.

Nick stood, as well, trying to get a glimpse of Joseph and her, but she pulled the door partly shut behind her. He answered his phone while he walked closer.

"What is it, Cooper?" he asked, knowing that was the only person who'd be calling him. Nick peered into the nursery and saw Kelly leaning over the crib. The baby stopped crying and began to babble instead.

The room was decorated with butterflies and birds. Bright primary colors. Kelly's artwork, no doubt. During the background check, he'd learned that she wasn't just a photographer but an artist, as well.

"I found a possible glitch," Cooper informed him.

Hell. This wasn't what he needed right now. "Go on." Nick kept his voice as soft as possible so he wouldn't alert Kelly. She took out the swab, mumbled something under her breath and then reached down toward the baby. Joseph made a protesting little sound and kicked at the covers.

"This one might be a real problem, sir," Cooper continued. "There's a P.I., a man named Denny Spencer. He was a close friend of Ms. Manning's late husband, and I think he might have been the one who buried her psych records. Anyway, yesterday he was poking through the police files that were retrieved from the Brighton Birthing Center—the place where both William and Joseph were born."

Nick watched as Kelly put the swab back into the sterile holder and laid it on the changing table. So, she'd gone through with it after all. There was no way she could know just how potentially critical, and dangerous, the DNA on that swab was. He needed to get it to a secure place as soon as possible.

"I don't think this Denny Spencer's made too many waves," Cooper explained. "*Yet.* But I think we need to silence him with a payoff. Or else I could set up a few obstacles to keep him occupied elsewhere."

"Neither." Nick left the rest unsaid. If Spencer was a friend of Kelly's, then it would only make the man more suspicious if someone tried to buy him off. "Put him under surveillance."

Kelly murmured something to the baby. Something with a soft, rhythmic cadence. It seemed to settle Joseph because his babblings no longer seemed to be of protest. He appeared to be trying to mimic what she was saying. It was a familiar activity since William and he did the same thing.

"Keep me informed," Nick told Cooper. He clicked off the phone in the middle of Cooper's goodbye and slipped it back into his pocket.

"It'll take me a couple of days to get back

William's DNA test," Kelly whispered from the nursery, snaring Nick's gaze from over her shoulder.

"You understand the need to keep all of this in the strictest confidence?" he asked.

"Of course."

Her assurance wasn't nearly enough. He'd take hers and Joseph's DNA samples before he left, and a private lab, one that he controlled, would do both tests. As a further precaution, he was the only person who would get the real results. Any information after that would be filtered through him. It wasn't an honest approach, but it could save Kelly Manning's life.

He glanced in the nursery again. Kelly took a diaper from the stack next to the crib and started to change Joseph. Nick managed to get just a glimpse of the boy. But that glimpse had his imagination racing.

Dark hair. Not brown. But black.

Nick's color.

Of course, plenty of babies had black hair.

Why couldn't he put this out of his mind? There was only the possibility that Meredith had lied to him. A *small* possibility, since to the best of his knowledge she hadn't lied to him about anything else. And she wouldn't have taken on something like this by herself if—

"Heck, you might as well come in," Kelly offered, interrupting his latest round of argument. "You've already given me a full body search, panties and all. Plus, I showed you my C-section scar. Seems a little late for modesty in the diapering department, doesn't it?"

It seemed a little late for a lot of things.

He took a few steps closer and stood in the doorway, but Nick didn't actually enter the room. It was best to keep some distance between them.

"You look shell-shocked. Did you get bad news from that phone call?" She looked away from him to continue diapering duty.

"Not really. Just a possible inconvenience."

Kelly made a sound of contemplation. Paused. And made another sound. "Have you given any more thought to me seeing William?"

"No." Not true. Nick had given it plenty of thought but decided it wasn't going to happen. "I figured after the test results—"

"That I'd slink away, carrying my lies with me? Wrong. Because, you see, I'm not lying. And as much as you distrust me, I don't trust you, either. You have the power and the money to doctor test results."

He couldn't possibly deny that because it was the truth. "You have the power and apparently the inclination to cause waves that shouldn't be made."

Her mouth went into a flat line. It was in contrast to the soft babbling sounds the baby was making. "I have a right to know if William is my son."

"And I have the right to protect him."

She huffed, finished diapering Joseph and turned to face him. "So we're back to where we started. Don't get me wrong, William's safety is important to me, too. But I'm just not convinced there are real issues here. I mean, if you've proven he's not your biological son, then why would he still be a threat to Eric?"

"Because as you so succinctly put, I have the power and the money to doctor test results."

"Did you?" she fired back.

"No."

Another huff but not an indignant one. This one was from frustration. "You know the truth, don't you?"

Best to go for the sarcastic approach again since she seemed to be very good at detecting lies. "I know many truths. Did you have one particular in mind?"

"*The* truth. About Joseph. Now, I want you to cut through all these evasive tactics and tell me what you know."

Nick stood there staring at her, but he couldn't stop the idea from dominating his thoughts. Meredith and he had been lovers. The timing was right. Plus, Meredith would have known about the danger of giving birth to his child.

"I'm still waiting for an answer," Kelly reminded him several moments later.

But he barely heard the reminder. Because at the exact moment she was speaking, the baby caught onto the crib railings and pulled himself to a standing position. He wore denim overalls and white cotton shirt. Joseph turned his head in Nick's direction, and just like that, their gazes connected.

Nick's breath froze in his lungs.

Joseph's face was round. Almost chubby. And he grinned. Just grinned. Showing his dimples.

Nick had seen photos of himself as a baby. But he didn't need the actual photo to know there was a strong resemblance.

"Meredith was your friend," Kelly continued. She scooped up the baby in her arms. "So you must have some idea of who Joseph's father is."

Yes.

Unfortunately, that idea wasn't a good one to voice. To anyone. Not even her. Just the hint of it would ultimately put all of them in danger. But it was especially dangerous for the child she held.

His child.

The heir he couldn't have.

Chapter Five

"Well?" Kelly prompted her visitor. He'd done it again—Nick had gone to la-la land while she was waiting for an answer to one of the most important questions she would ever ask.

He blew off her question and headed for the kitchen. "I need a drink of water."

Before she could follow him, Nick opened several cabinet doors, located a glass and helped himself to some tap water. He certainly looked as if he needed it, too. And was it her imagination that he looked a little shell-shocked? Kelly didn't let that prevent her from pressing for an answer.

"Do you know who Joseph's father is?" she asked.

Nick set his now empty glass on the counter and looked her straight in the eye. "No."

She frowned. "That's scary, you know that?"

"What?"

"Lying while maintaining direct eye contact. A lot

of people wouldn't be able to do it, yet you managed it with surprising ease."

Now he frowned. "Who says I'm lying?"

"Me." Kelly planted a kiss on Joseph's cheek. "Meredith trusted you enough to raise her son. I can't believe she wouldn't tell you who the father is."

"Perhaps I'm keeping a confidence that Meredith asked me to keep."

Kelly nodded and shifted Joseph to her left hip. She went closer to Nick. "Yes. I thought of that, even though I can't imagine why a dying woman would want to keep something like that a secret."

"She had her reasons, I'm sure."

That was all he apparently intended to offer. It was a clear signal that her mini-interrogation was over. Well, it was over as far as he was concerned. Kelly made sure Nick noticed her frown when she walked past him on the way to the pantry. Too bad she didn't give him a wide enough berth. Her left breast grazed him. Hardly enough for her to notice.

But she noticed.

It sent a strange, unwanted curl of heat through her body, that she quickly pushed aside.

Figuring he had a new playmate, Joseph reached for their guest, specifically the buttons on his white shirt. Kelly managed to step away before Joseph could latch on.

Her visitor certainly wasn't exactly dressed like a

wrangling cowboy, though she knew for a fact that he was a real rancher. He wore a black suit. A suit that fitted his butt, thighs and chest extremely well.

And she hated that she'd allowed herself to notice something like that.

The suit wasn't exactly stodgy, either. It was as expensive as they came and it had a GQ look to it. His white dress shirt was unbuttoned at the throat and upper chest, and he wore it as naturally and easily as he had his tux. She figured he'd be equally at home in his cowboy clothes and had a minifantasy about how he'd look in jeans.

Hot, no doubt.

Kelly mentally kicked herself. Jeans fantasies. Mercy, she was definitely not thinking straight.

Nick followed her to the pantry, carrying his undeniable presence with him. Why did the kitchen suddenly seem so small?

She took out a jar of toddler food, grabbed a spoon and bib and was about to put Joseph in his high chair when the phone rang. Cradling the phone between her ear and shoulder, she gave Joseph an adjustment on her hip. He didn't seem to like that because he fussed.

"Kelly?" It was Denny Spencer, and just from that one-word greeting, she could tell that he didn't sound pleased. "Is Nick Lattimer there?"

Only because she wasn't up to an argument—and there would be an argument—she considered lying.

But in all likelihood, Denny had already seen Nick's car. Hence the reason for the call.

"He's here," Kelly verified.

She met Nick's granite, blue-gray gaze when she answered. He lifted his eyebrow. A question, of sorts. Kelly ignored him and turned away. However, she couldn't ignore Denny. He immediately started to curse.

"Have you lost your mind?" Denny demanded.

"I just want the truth," Kelly reminded him.

"Well, you won't get that from Nick Lattimer. He's doing everything he can to stop you. And *me,*" Denny insisted.

Kelly was about to ask what he meant by that, but Joseph fussed even louder. She tried to slide off the high chair tray so she could get her son seated, but Joseph didn't cooperate with that, either.

Nick came to the rescue.

As if he'd done it a thousand times, and maybe he had, he took off the tray, eased Joseph from her arms and deposited the baby onto the seat.

"Finish your call," Nick insisted.

Kelly's first instinct was to say no, but Nick just took over. He snatched up the bib, put it on Joseph and proceeded to feed him. She would have protested if he hadn't been so darn good at what he was doing. And if Joseph hadn't stopped fussing. Not only did he stop, her son began to wolf down the baby beef stew mixture, and he gave Nick the reward of a grin.

Only because she was watching the two so closely did she see the softness in Nick Lattimer's eyes.

Yes, softness!

It was both surprising and a little frightening. Because that wasn't the look of a care giver. It was the look of someone who genuinely loved children. She prayed that didn't mean he would give her a custody fight to keep William.

"Did you hear me?" Denny snarled.

Actually, she hadn't. "Could I call you back? Things are a little hectic right now."

That earned her another raised eyebrow from Nick, probably because it was a lie. Joseph had settled nicely into his feeding and wasn't fussing.

"No. You can't call me back," Denny countered. "You need to hear this, and when you do, I'll come over there and throw Nick Lattimer out of your house."

Since Denny was talking quite loudly and since she didn't want Nick to overhear any part of this conversation, Kelly walked toward the nursery. She didn't close the door because she wanted to keep an eye on her baby, but she did lower her voice to a whisper.

"What do I need to hear?" she asked.

"I've been investigating what went on at the Brighton Birthing Center, but suddenly everyone is stonewalling me. I can't get access to the records, and no one is talking. One guess as to who's responsible for that—Nick Lattimer."

Kelly couldn't deny it. Her visitor certainly had the power and resources for stonewalling. Better yet, he had a motive. He thought all of this digging for the truth would alert his brother, Eric. And that brought her to something that could put an end to any possible threat from Eric Lattimer.

"Denny, could you drop by in about a half hour?" She glanced at Nick and Joseph to verify that the feeding was still going well. It was. And Kelly looked at the trio of buccal swab kits on the changing table. "I need you to take a DNA sample to a lab."

He didn't answer right away. "Lattimer actually agreed to give you DNA from his ward?"

"Yes."

Silence. Kelly welcomed it because it gave her a moment to think, something she hadn't had time to do since the moment Nick had stepped into her house. Did Nick's willingness to give her the sample mean that he was sure there hadn't been a baby swap? Or like her, did he simply want to know the truth?

But she immediately rethought that last question.

Nick and she had zero trust between them. So, why would he have given her the very thing that she could ultimately use to take William from him? Judging from the way he was gazing at Joseph, he loved kids. She had no doubts that he loved William. So why was he making it easy for her?

Or was he?

She eyed the empty water glass on her kitchen counter. "I want you to have something else tested," she whispered to Denny. "A glass. I want the DNA on it compared to Nick Lattimer and William. Will you take care of that for me?"

"You know I will, but that doesn't answer the question about Lattimer himself. You shouldn't be there alone with him, Kelly. He's dangerous—"

"I know. I'll be careful."

And with that, she hung up because she knew that Denny was about to launch into round two of his argument. She appreciated his concern. She truly did. But more than concern, Kelly needed to know the truth. If William was her son, then she needed to prove that and get him away from Nick. That, in turn, would assure that he'd be safe from Nick's brother.

Kelly grabbed Joseph's DNA test and her own from the changing table and walked back into the kitchen so she could place the phone into its cradle. Joseph was on the last few bites of his lunch, and he seemed to be enjoying the attention from this stranger. Ditto for the stranger. Nick didn't even react when Joseph splattered some of the beef stew onto his white shirt.

She automatically reached for a paper towel,

dampened one end and began to wipe away the blob. Not the best idea she'd ever had. Because it meant she was wiping Nick's chest.

He was solid, but then, she already had proof of that when he searched her at the ranch. However, it seemed more intimate touching him now.

She stepped back as if he'd scalded her.

He snared her gaze and reached out to her. For a moment Kelly thought he might touch her. And for a moment, one crazy insane moment, she thought she might like that. But he didn't touch. He merely took Joseph's and her DNA test kits from her hand and slipped them into his jacket pocket.

"Your P.I. friend warned you about me," Nick announced.

"Yes." Though she had no idea how he'd known that it was Denny on the phone. Despite his uncanny knack for identifying a caller, Kelly was thankful for the conversation. Anything to distance her from the reaction she'd just had to him. "Denny's worried about me."

"Your friend has a reason to worry. If you continue to press for this DNA evidence, you're only putting yourself in more danger."

"I don't believe that."

"You should," he warned.

He didn't get a chance to say more because his cell phone rang. Kelly took over the feeding duties. Not that there was much left to do. She gave Joseph the last spoonful and wiped his face. She took his from the high chair while she tried to eavesdrop on Nick's call.

But eavesdropping was useless.

The man spoke in single-syllable responses, even though she was certain this was a conversation that was important.

Nick was a pacer. He moved across her kitchen and into the adjoining family room. And he paced. Not some awkward, angry gait. He was smooth. Interesting. With his pricy suit and rugged but somehow aristocratic face. He was a man accustomed to wielding power.

The sunlight from the windows was amber clear and at the perfect angle to bathe him in light. When he paused by the fireplace, Kelly had the sudden urge to shoot him. With her camera, that is. She could use a 135mm range with one added stop of exposure. Fast-speed film would be more forgiving, but with a slower-speed film, she could capture every nuance of that gritty intensity. That face. Those incredible features.

And she had to remind herself—again—that while the Italian-suit-wearing rancher might make a good photographic subject, she should not be referring to any of his features as *incredible*.

He finished his call and put his phone back into his pocket. She waited for an explanation of what had caused the pacing and the intensity, but he didn't provide her with one.

"I want you to consider staying at my ranch until we have the test results."

Kelly wouldn't have been more surprised if he'd stepped into a song and dance. "Excuse me?"

"It's for your safety."

But he wasn't looking at her. He was looking at Joseph. And then he did something else that surprised her. He reached out and touched his index finger to Joseph's cheek.

Alarms the size of Texas went off in her head. Because that wasn't the look of concern.

It was the look of a father.

But it couldn't be.

Could it?

She immediately considered the ramifications of that. No, it couldn't be.

"I can't go to your ranch," she managed to say, though how she didn't know. Kelly could hardly catch her breath.

She took Joseph from the high chair and headed toward the nursery. Of course Nick followed.

"What's wrong?" he asked.

"Nothing," she lied.

But everything was wrong. Well, everything if Nick, Meredith or both had told the ultimate lie.

Mercy, was he really Joseph's father?

Kelly couldn't help it. She glanced at both of them. The hair was the most noticeable similarity.

But then, black was a common hair color. And they didn't have the same color eyes. Nick's were stormy gray, and Joseph's were more blue. Though there were times when they looked gray, as well. Still, those two things meant nothing.

And then her son smiled, showing those precious dimples. Kelly had seen that smile hundreds of times, and she'd cherished every one of them. But it was Nick's reaction that she didn't cherish.

He smiled, too.

At Joseph.

Nick's dimples flashed, too.

She couldn't dismiss those dimples. It was as if a brick wall had fallen on her. Kelly couldn't breathe, and she felt on the verge of a panic attack. She hadn't had one for nearly two years, not since the night her husband was killed, but she didn't think she could fight it off this time.

Things started to move fast. Her heart. Her thoughts. The blood in her veins. Everything seemed to be racing out of control, and she couldn't catch on to anything to anchor herself.

Kelly grabbed the jacket that she'd left on the counter, coiled it around Joseph and headed for the back porch. "I need some fresh air," she insisted.

And she needed some privacy so she could deal with this. Kelly stepped onto the back porch and shut the door behind her.

Thankfully, this time Nick didn't follow.

Because she couldn't stop, because she couldn't stay still, she wrapped the jacket tightly around Joseph and hurried out into the backyard. It was a peaceful place. Two white bird fountains and red granite rock beds. In the background, the massive live oaks were still sporting their emerald leaves and were swaying in the breeze.

The serene scenery and the cold air helped. But nothing could stop her thoughts. If Meredith had lied and Nick was indeed Joseph's father, then…

But Kelly couldn't even let herself finish that.

God, why hadn't she seen the resemblance between Joseph and Nick sooner? Why had she put all of this into motion by going to Nick Lattimer?

Her quest for the truth could ultimately cost her Joseph.

And what about William?

Kelly couldn't begin to deal with the idea of trading one child for another. All along she'd thought she would have both boys.

But Nick might not have the same idea.

The tears came. They burned hot in her eyes as the wind assaulted her face. But even through the tears, she saw the flicker of motion, and it grabbed her attention.

It came from the back of her property. From what was commonly called the greenbelt. The trees were thick there but not so thick that she didn't see something that she didn't want to see.

A man.

He was dressed all in black and had a ski mask covering his face. Kelly turned to run, but it was too late.

The man charged right at her.

NICK GROANED and leaned his back against the door.

He wanted to kick himself where it hurt most. So much for his infamous iceman expression. He obviously hadn't been icy when he looked at Joseph. No. He'd been all fire and emotion because he hadn't been able to hide his fear that this precious little boy might be his son.

And now Kelly was suspicious.

At best, Kelly and he had a tenuous relationship. Neither trusted the other. This revelation was likely to cause her distrust to skyrocket. With reason. She was probably out there right now wondering if he was going to take the child she'd raised as her own.

Nick was wondering the same thing.

What the hell was he going to do?

It would have been so easy to blame Meredith for not telling him the truth and for somehow arranging for the babies to be switched. But he couldn't do that. Because deep inside, Nick knew if she'd lied, then her lie hadn't been one of deception but protection. If Eric had learned that Meredith had given birth to Nick's heir, then the baby would have been assassinated.

Of course, Eric hadn't known about the baby. Neither had Nick. If he had, he would have done everything humanly possible to stop his brother, so that Eric couldn't get to the child. But Meredith hadn't told him so that he could help her. Instead, she'd taken care of the situation herself.

His son was alive because of Meredith's lie. Because she'd had the courage to give her child to another woman so his DNA wouldn't be linked to the Lattimer line. But that lie had also involved Kelly and her son in all of this.

Nick groaned again, wished he had something to punch and whirled around to check on Kelly.

His heart slammed to the floor.

With Joseph gripped in her arms, Kelly was frantically running for the door. She wasn't alone. There was a man in a ski mask chasing them.

Not one man, Nick quickly corrected.

But two.

He saw the second one race out from the side yard.

Nick did some racing, too. He reached in the back waist of his pants and pulled out a snub-nosed .38. He jerked open the door and headed out. He had to get there in time. He couldn't watch Kelly and Joseph gunned down before his eyes.

"Help me," Kelly shouted.

Nick did his best to do just that. He jumped off the porch, landing hard on the ground, and he quickly maneuvered himself between Kelly and the men.

"Get inside," Nick ordered her.

She didn't argue. He heard her barrel up the steps, but Nick kept his focus on the two men. The one who'd come from the side yard lifted his gun and took aim at Kelly.

Nick took aim, too. At the man. He was ready to kill if necessary, but the other man didn't fire. He must have realized that he was about to be shot because he turned and started to run. So did his comrade.

So did Nick.

He raced toward the men, hoping to capture just one of them so he could beat some answers out of them. And the men were definitely fools if they'd decided to take him on.

Nick tackled the man, and they both went crashing to the ground. He was ready to slug the guy, but the sound stopped Nick cold.

Someone fired a shot.

Nick glanced up and spotted the other man. He'd taken aim not at Nick but at the house. Where Kelly and Joseph were still standing.

The anger raged through Nick, and he brought up his weapon so he could return fire. But it was too late. The man ducked behind some trees. Worse, Nick saw the movement out of the corner of his eye a split second before he felt his captive's elbow slam into his jaw.

"Move and they die," someone yelled. It was the man at the back of the yard.

Nick glanced at the house and saw Kelly and Joseph still on the porch. She was struggling to get the back door open.

Since the elbow shot had thrown off Nick's aim and position and since he couldn't risk Kelly and Joseph being shot, Nick froze. His captive didn't. The man sprang to his feet and started to run toward his comrade.

Both men disappeared into the woods.

Nick wanted to run after them. But he couldn't. He couldn't leave Kelly and Joseph alone.

He hurried to the porch, and Kelly got the door open just as he joined her. Nick rushed her and the baby inside, locked the door and took out his cell phone.

"Are you hurt?" Nick asked.

She shook her head but didn't say anything. With her breath coming out in rough, jagged gusts, Kelly just stared at him. So did Joseph. The little boy had shoved the jacket from his head, and he looked as if he didn't know whether to smile or cry.

Nick checked the baby for any sign of injury and didn't see any. Well, no visible signs, anyway. He silently cursed the men who'd put Joseph through this.

He called 911 and requested police assistance. He

made a second call to the security guard he'd posted up the street. For all the good it'd done. But he wanted the guard here at the house in case the gunmen made a return visit.

"Those men wanted to kill us," Kelly whispered.

Because she seemed on the verge of collapsing, Nick slid his arm around her and pulled her to him. "For what it's worth, I don't think they had murder on their minds."

Blinking back tears, she looked up at him. "Then, what did they want?"

"I think this might have been a kidnapping attempt. If they'd wanted to kill you, they would have stayed in the cover of the trees and fired the shots."

From that range, they wouldn't have missed.

"And the one shot they did fire at you was well over your head. I think it went into the roof," he added.

He watched her process that in the depth of her cool green eyes. She didn't process it well. "You think they wanted information or something?"

Or something.

And Nick had a sickening feeling that the *something* was Joseph.

He looked down at her and didn't pull any punches. "Those men could come back. Next time you might not be so lucky. This isn't really a request, Kelly. You and Joseph are moving in with me at the ranch. And we're leaving *now*."

Chapter Six

Kelly's emotions were all over the place. On the one hand, going to Nick's ranch wasn't on the top of her list of fun things to do. But on the other hand, Joseph would be safe. And she'd be under the same roof as William.

She would finally get a chance to see him.

That outweighed the negative part about being Nick's "houseguest."

"This way," Nick instructed leading her through the maze of hallways that made up the main ranch house. It was nearly eight thousand square feet of space, but it felt twice that size.

Kelly followed him, as she'd done since they'd left her house after the police had come and questioned them. She hoped she wasn't making another mistake by blindly obeying Nick. And by coming to his ranch. However, no matter what she did, it was a risk, especially considering the chaos that'd come from her last visit here. She might be in danger of losing Joseph, and they might be in danger, period.

Someone had tried to kidnap them.

Or maybe worse.

It was that threat that had prompted Kelly to move in with Nick. But once she knew the truth about William and had a workable plan to get custody of him, she would take her sons and get out of there. Well, she would do that after she made arrangements for security, that is. The boys' safety had to be her top priority.

"This is your suite," Nick announced, throwing open a set of double doors.

While she kept a firm hold on Joseph, she walked inside. Kelly had expected luxury. After all, Nick was wealthy. But she hadn't expected it to feel homey, and that's exactly how the room was. Decorated in varying shades of blue, there was a fireplace and French doors that led to an enclosed glass patio. She had a perfect view of the sun setting on the garden.

"Joseph's nursery is through there," Nick said, pointing to the door on the other side of the room. "The nanny, Greta, is available to watch him anytime you need."

"Yes. I met her the night of the party. She's William's nanny." It wasn't a question. It was a hint that she wanted to see her son.

"She is," Nick verified. He deposited her suitcase in the massive walk-in closet.

Kelly waited until he'd finished that task before she caught his arm. So did Joseph. And he giggled when Nick smiled at him and goosed his belly. It was a tender, light moment at a time when her situation seemed pretty dark.

Since Nick hadn't responded to her hint, she decided to go with the direct approach. "I want to see William," Kelly said.

He didn't answer her right away, but she could see the debate stirring his jaw muscles. "Later. Right now I have to make some calls. Get settled in, and I'll be back to take you to the nursery."

Kelly hadn't thought she could get even more emotional, but that did it. She had to blink to fight back the tears, and her heart seemed to swell with the anticipation of finally being able to see her child. Not on a monitor this time.

"Thank you," she whispered.

Nick looked at Joseph, mumbled something under his breath and made a hasty exit.

Kelly welcomed the reprieve. She hadn't had a moment to herself since the attempted kidnapping. Plus, she had her own phone call to make. She sat on the thickly carpeted floor so that Joseph could crawl around, and she took her phone from her diaper bag. She dialed Denny Spencer's number.

He answered on the first ring and obviously saw her name on his caller ID. "Kelly, where the heck are you?"

She avoided answering that. "Someone tried to kidnap Joseph and me."

"Yes, I know. When I went to your house, the police were still there, and I talked to them. They said you'd left with Nick Lattimer."

Oops. Denny knew. So there wasn't any way to avoid this. "I did. He saved our lives."

Denny made a sound to indicate he didn't believe that. "Are you sure he wasn't the one who sent those gunmen after you?"

Kelly was more than a little surprised with that particular question. "Why would he do that?"

"To get you to trust him."

"Again—why would he do that?" Kelly didn't wait for an answer. "Look, I don't trust him, Denny. Not completely. But I believe he's capable of protecting Joseph. Right now that's my main priority."

"I can protect Joseph as well as he can," Denny insisted. His insistence had a territorial ring to it. She was aware that Denny cared for her on much more than a professional level, but he was also aware that nothing personal could ever happen between them.

Kelly pulled in a deep, weary breath. "The ranch has security, Denny. We'll be safe here until I can figure out what's going on."

"And you'll get to see William," he fired back. "That's the real reason you're there. Kelly, what if he's not yours? What if all of this has been some dangerous wild-goose chase?"

She didn't believe that. "That's why I need the DNA tests done."

"I know. I've already taken the glass and the swab with William's DNA to the lab. I picked them up while I was at your house."

"Oh, God. I can't believe I left the swab there." But then, she hadn't exactly been thinking straight after the confrontation with those gunmen.

"I also took the lab some of Joseph's hairs that I got from his brush," Denny continued.

Kelly's heart sank, and she put her hand on her chest to steady it. With Joseph's DNA, the lab could compare it to Nick's. And that could be a very bad thing. "The results have to stay confidential," Kelly warned.

"They will. The lab tech is a friend and will put a rush on all three tests. You'll get preliminary results in a day or two, but if you want something that'll stand up in court, you'll need to wait for a different set of tests."

"The preliminary ones are fine for now," Kelly insisted. She only hoped she could live with the consequences of what she'd already set into motion.

"You can thank me by getting away from Nick Lattimer," Denny countered.

"Soon, Denny. I promise. Once I have the lab results, I can clear up a lot of things."

And she could muddy the waters beyond belief, too. But she'd deal with that later. Right now she wanted to see William.

Kelly ended the call, picked up Joseph and went in search of either Nick or the nanny. Maybe she could see William. She didn't find the nanny, but it didn't take her long before she heard Nick's voice. She followed the sound of it to the end of the hall and found him standing behind a massive desk in his office. He had his jacket slung over the back of the chair and had loosened another button on his shirt.

"I repeat—are you responsible for that kidnapping attempt?" she heard Nick demand.

That captured her full attention, and Kelly stopped just outside the door.

"Why would I want to kidnap her?" the caller responded. It was a man, and his cold hard voice came through over the speakerphone.

Kelly had no doubt that this was the infamous Eric.

"Don't play games with me," Nick warned. He bracketed his hands on his desk and learned closer to the phone. Every muscle in his body seemed primed and ready for a fight. "You have no reason to be interested in Kelly Manning."

"Oh, but I do. I'm interested because you're interested in her. I like to keep watch on you, little brother."

That chilled her to the bone. Not just the sinister

voice, but the implication. God, was he admitting to the kidnapping attempt?

Joseph babbled something and reached for the door frame. The sound must have alerted Nick because he looked up. Caught her gaze. The tension was there, all over his face.

"Kelly Manning and I are having an affair," Nick lied. "It's just sex between us. Nothing more. And we have no plans to produce an heir. So you don't have any reason to feel threatened by her."

"Threatened?" Eric apparently took that as the ultimate insult. "Hardly. I'm simply cautious."

"You're paranoid," Nick countered. "Honestly, Eric, get a life. That's what I'm trying to do."

"With Kelly Manning," he concluded. "Well, she's attractive—I'll give her that. How's she in bed? She doesn't look like the missionary type. I'll bet she's a biter and a scratcher."

"That's none of your damn business." She saw his knuckles turn white from the pressure he was exerting against the desk. "Eric, if you do anything to harm either Kelly or her son, then you're a dead man. That's not a threat, either. It's a guarantee. I'll come after you with everything I have."

Eric laughed, but Kelly could hear no humor in it. "What about the promise you made to our dying mother not to do me any harm?"

"It's a promise I'll break if you come near them."

Another humorless laugh. "Have a good evening, Nick." And Eric hung up.

Nick pressed the end call button. "I told him we were having an affair so it would explain why we're spending time together. Maybe it'll stop him from doing anything else stupid."

Kelly walked closer to him. "So, you think he tried to kidnap us?"

"He's the only person with motive."

Yes. She couldn't dispute that. "Would you really kill him?"

But an answer wasn't necessary. Nick would do it. For Joseph and her, even though they were practically strangers. That realization blended with the attraction she already felt for him. Whatever this weird feeling was, it couldn't get stronger. She'd already learned the hard way not to get involved with a dangerous man.

And Nick was as dangerous as they came.

Joseph began to squirm to get down, and Kelly soon spotted the source of his interest. He was reaching for the shiny silver picture frame on Nick's desk. Except it wasn't a frame she soon realized. It was a small video monitoring screen.

Of the nursery.

To get a better look, Kelly moved closer. So close that she was practically touching Nick. Joseph apparently liked the closeness. He reached out and began to examine Nick's white rolled-up shirtsleeve. Kelly gave Joseph a kiss on the cheek and watched the screen.

She soon saw the nanny cross the room. And she was carrying William in her arms. The little boy was wearing pale-blue pants and a matching top.

Kelly's breath stalled in her throat.

She latched on to that image, committing every small detail to memory. William's blond hair. The shape of his face. His mouth that was bent into a smile.

Everything inside her screamed that this was her son.

"I just had my security manager send the DNA in for testing," she heard Nick say.

Kelly didn't tell him that Denny had done the same. Soon they would all know the truth. In the meantime, her heart was aching to get a better look at the little boy on the screen.

Joseph continued to squirm, but the monitor no longer held his attention. It was Nick that he wanted. Her son reached for the man, but Kelly stepped away to put some distance between them. She only wished she could add some emotional distance, as well.

"I want to see William," Kelly requested.

She expected Nick to stonewall her again. In fact, she braced herself to hear an unequivocal no.

That didn't happen.

"Follow me," Nick said.

But that wasn't all he did.

Joseph reached for him again, and this time Nick closed the distance between them and reached right back. He took the baby out of her arms before Kelly even realized what was happening.

"This way," Nick instructed.

Carrying Joseph in his arms, Nick walked out of his office and down the hall. Kelly followed. Somehow. Though just watching him hold Joseph put her heart into a tailspin.

NICK FIGURED this was a mistake, but it was one that he couldn't avoid making. Kelly wasn't just going to give up the idea of seeing William.

And Nick wasn't sure he had the right to deny her.

Things were moving fast. Too fast. And with the danger from Eric hanging over them like the Sword of Damocles, he had a lot on his mind. But first and foremost were the two boys. If Joseph was indeed his son, that meant Kelly was likely William's biological mother. It cut his heart in two to know that he could lose the boy to Kelly. But it cut just as deeply that he might have a son he could never claim.

Hell, what a tangled web Meredith had spun if she'd indeed arranged a baby switch. Of course, Nick couldn't blame her if she had. If their situations had been reversed, he might have done the same. In fact, he would do anything to protect the son he'd come to love as his own and the son who might indeed be his.

Joseph seemed perfectly content in his arms and was babbling things to him as they trekked down the hall. Occasionally the boy's attention would land on a painting, and he'd purse his mouth into an "ohhh" and point at it.

Nick couldn't resist. When they stopped outside the nursery doors, he kissed the boy on his forehead.

Kelly saw him, and she was probably aware that she frowned. Nick figured there'd be a lot more frowns and groans before they got to the truth. And even after. He didn't have a clue how they were going to resolve this.

"One step at a time," he heard Kelly say.

"For what?" he asked, wondering if she'd read his mind or if she was giving herself advice.

But she only shook her head and frowned again.

Nick opened the doors to the nursery. He took a deep breath. And he waited to see what Kelly would do. He didn't have to wait long.

The nanny, Greta, was in her rocking chair, and William was on the floor playing with his toys. Kelly walked toward him. Cautiously. And she stooped down so that she'd be at his level. William eyed her warily and looked to Nick for some kind of assurance that this stranger was okay.

"Hey, buddy," Nick said to William. That earned him a beaming smile, and William began to pound the floor with the stuffed dog that he had clutched in his hand.

"Da-da," William said.

Joseph must have listened and learned because he quickly repeated it:

"Da-da."

Nick required another deep breath after hearing that. So did Kelly. In fact, she turned pale and sank down on the floor next to William. Tears sprang to her eyes. The nanny must have sensed something important was going on because she excused herself and closed the door behind her.

Still babbling "Da-da," Joseph squirmed to get out of Nick's arms. Nick deposited him on the floor, and Joseph toddled toward his new found playmate and the stash of toys.

Using Kelly's arm, William pulled himself to a standing position and walked the rest of the way toward Joseph. The boys were nearly the same height and weight. Both could obviously walk and say a few words. But that's where the similarities ended. William had curly blond hair and blue-green eyes. Joseph's black locks were board-straight and on the wild side, and he had the Lattimer intensity down pat.

Kelly caught on to William's hand and tried to encourage him to go into her arms, but William wanted no part of that. Even though it went against what his heart wanted him to do, Nick eased down on the floor with the three of them. He caught William and turned him in Kelly's direction.

She slid her arms around William and pulled him to her.

Her green eyes weren't just tear filled. The tears began to stream down her cheeks. Joseph got in on the action. He snuggled into Kelly's arms, too, and soon she held both boys.

"Thank you," she mumbled. And Nick realized she was talking to him.

The boys quickly grew tired of the hugging and broke away so they could play with a stack of wooden blocks. Kelly and Nick sat there and watched. Well, he watched until he realized that Kelly's tears weren't going to stop anytime soon. He scooted next to her, took out his handkerchief and handed it to her.

"William looks like me," she said. Her teary gaze met his. "And don't you dare deny it."

He couldn't, even though he wanted to.

She didn't say a word about Joseph looking like him.

"I didn't think I'd feel this way," she continued. "I've lost thirteen months with him, and it hurts so much that I don't think I can stand it."

Nick had no trouble understanding that.

"What are we going to do?" she asked.

"We're going to learn the truth."

Kelly shook her head. "And then what?"

Nick didn't know. Other than trying to protect all of them, he had no idea what they were about to face.

"Greta, the nanny, will help you get settled in," Nick instructed. He stood. "Get some rest. We'll talk about this in the morning."

He only hoped by then he had some answers that could keep them all alive.

Chapter Seven

Nick downed his third cup of black coffee and hoped the caffeine would kick in soon. He had a wicked headache from lack of sleep, and he needed all the help he could get to feel alert and awake.

Sitting at his desk, he finalized the purchase of a prize Santa Gertrudis bull, signed some payroll checks and then got to work on what was really important.

Beefing up security.

He left an e-memo for Cooper to add more cameras and motion detectors to the perimeter of the ranch. It wouldn't be foolproof, but he had to do something to make sure that nothing happened to Kelly and Joseph. That kidnapping attempt had shaken her to the core, and he couldn't have a repeat of that.

He glanced at the monitor when he saw some movement on the screen, and he spotted Kelly and Greta with the babies. They'd probably just finished bathing and feeding them. Kelly kissed both Joseph and William, she said something to Greta, and she left the room.

Nick did some adjustments to the camera and watched her walk up the hall toward his office. She'd obviously showered and dressed. She wore black pants and a green top. A snug top that made him notice her breasts.

Of course, everything she wore caused him to notice her breasts and her other interesting features. In the few hours he'd managed to sleep, he'd dreamed about her. During his waking hours, he'd thought about her, too. A lot.

"Come in," Nick told her when she knocked on his door. He switched the camera back to the nursery. Best not to let Kelly see that he'd been watching her.

Looking a little unsure of herself, Kelly stepped inside. Nick saw it then. The fatigue. Specifically, the dark smudgy shadows beneath her eyes. She obviously hadn't slept much, either.

He motioned toward the coffee carafe on his desk, and she helped herself to a cup. "Thanks. I had some at breakfast, but I could sure use some more."

And she downed several gulps but didn't say anything else. Still, it was obvious that she had something on her mind, or she wouldn't have left the babies to come to his office.

"Is something wrong?" Nick finally asked.

"Dreams," she said peering at him from over the

rim of the coffee cup. "Well, nightmares, anyway. I keep reliving the kidnapping attempt."

"That's natural, I suppose." God knows, he'd relived it.

"I also kept thinking about what we're going to do. We don't really have a plan other than to wait and see. And with what happened yesterday, it feels as if we need a lot more than that."

Because he was a man accustomed to solving problems, he nearly offered the obvious—*I'll take care of everything.* But they had no choice but to wait and pray that the danger was something they could handle. He certainly couldn't promise her that all would be well.

She walked closer and looked down at him. Despite the sleep-starved eyes, she was alert and obviously had something else on her mind. "Whatever the DNA results say, you won't just give William up, will you?"

"No." Nick didn't even have to think about it. William was his son, even if they didn't share the same DNA.

Kelly nodded, and she set her cup back onto the serving tray. Her hand and her bottom lip were trembling. Nick wasn't immune to it, either. This situation was breaking her heart. And his.

Knowing it was a mistake and not caring, Nick stood, eased his arm around her and pulled her to him.

Kelly froze and looked at him. "You're not going to frisk me again, are you?"

Nick couldn't help it. He smiled. "No." But unfortunately, the closeness automatically gave him ideas about her that he shouldn't have.

She stared at him, blinking back tears. Nick stared at her, too. In fact, he couldn't seem to take his eyes off her. She was attractive. Beautiful, even. And his reaction to her seemed to be growing by leaps and bounds.

He reached in his pocket, offered her another handkerchief. and Kelly used it to blot away the tears. "This is a little too cozy for comfort."

"I agree." He started to move away from her, but she settled against him as if it were the most natural thing in the world.

It felt natural.

But wrong. Any kind of emotional entanglement could complicate the heck out of things.

"Part of me says I shouldn't trust you," she whispered. "The other part of me is thankful that you're here to protect Joseph and William."

Oh, yeah. They were definitely on the same page.

He looked down at her just as she looked up at him. Something happened.

A stir of energy.

A change in heart rates and breathing patterns. That look was more potent than a heavyweight's fist, and his body quickly reminded him that he was a man. And that Kelly was a woman.

Nick wanted to kiss her. And suddenly that seemed just as important as his next breath.

Kelly didn't look away. Nick had no idea why he couldn't veto the really stupid thoughts that his body was suggesting that he do.

She lifted her head. He lowered his. And he brushed her mouth with his. It was just a touch. Barely a kiss. But it caused a massive reaction. She jerked away from him and slapped her palm against his chest.

"I can't," she said.

Nick welcomed those words. They were like music to his ears. Because he should have said it, as well. Thankfully, she'd done it for him.

She crammed her hands in the pockets of her pants. "I'm attracted to you," she admitted. Then, she shook her head as if disgusted with herself.

He considered lying, but after that semikiss, the truth was way too obvious. "I'm attracted to you, too."

Kelly paused a moment. "I had a bad marriage. *Really* bad. In fact, the last thing I said to my husband were words shouted in anger." She groaned. "And I have no idea why I just told you that because that has nothing to do with anything happening here."

"You told me because of this weird intimacy between us," Nick explained. "It's the danger. The adrenaline and the fear make strange bedfellows."

He mentally winced at his choice of words, but it caused her to smile. Only, it faded as quickly as it'd come. Nick hated that, because it had made him feel good just to be on the receiving end of a smile like that.

"We have a difficult road ahead of us. It's probably best if we stay…as neutral as possible toward each other," she said.

True. But Nick knew that was impossible. Already the barriers were breaking down.

"You have visitors," Cooper informed him over the intercom. "Paula Barker and Todd Burgess. They're waiting for you in the solarium."

Nick huffed and finished off his cup of coffee. He'd need the final jolt of caffeine for this particular meeting.

"Are they cops?" Kelly asked.

"No." But Nick had to see them. If they'd come to the ranch, then it had to be important. Hell. He didn't need anything else on his plate.

Kelly caught his arm when he started to leave. "I don't know how to sugarcoat this, so I'm just going to come out and ask you for the truth. Do you believe that you're Joseph's biological father?"

Nick didn't have a quick answer for that. Yes, he believed he was, but there was no way he was going to admit it. Not to her. Not to anyone.

There was another slight crackle of sound, and Nick heard Cooper's voice again over the intercom. "Sir?"

"I'm on the way to the solarium now," Nick informed him. He headed for the door.

"You have another visitor," Cooper said.

That stopped Nick in his tracks. "Who?"

"Your brother, Eric. He's here on the front porch, and he's demanding to see you now."

KELLY HURRIED out of Nick's office and caught up with him while he was practically storming down the hall. "Does your brother come here often?" she asked.

"Never."

Well, that didn't do much to steady her suddenly raw nerves. It also didn't help when Nick checked the gun he had tucked in a slide holster in the back of his jeans.

"I don't want you to be around when I talk to Eric," Nick insisted.

Kelly considered his order, mainly because hiding would be the easy and safe thing to do. But Eric was the man who likely tried to kidnap Joseph and her. She didn't want to hide; she wanted to confront him.

Cooper was waiting at the front door. He had his gun drawn, and he gave her a questioning glance.

"I have a right to be here," Kelly told him. "This involves me."

Nick stopped so abruptly that she nearly ran right into him, and he turned and took her by the shoulders. She could tell that he was about to launch into an argument as to why she shouldn't come face-to-face with Eric. But Kelly gave her own argument before he could.

"I can reassure Eric that I have no plans to produce your heir, and I can convince him to leave Joseph and me alone." She hoped. Kelly wasn't certain she could convince the man of anything, but she wanted the chance to confront him.

"I'm not leaving," she added. "Not when there's this much at stake."

Nick obviously didn't care about her argument. He moved her into the adjacent sitting room. "Eric's capable of murder," was all Nick said. He also motioned for Cooper to join her so they could make sure that she stayed put.

Kelly did, sort of. She maneuvered herself to Cooper's other side so she could see their visitor's re-flection in the mirror of the rosewood umbrella stand in the foyer. Nick opened the door, and Kelly realized she had a perfect view of the man who might be trying to terrorize her.

He certainly didn't look like a killer.

In fact, he looked like Nick.

No one would doubt they were brothers. They had the same midnight-black hair. The same strongly angled jaw. The same olive-toned skin. But that's where the similarities ended. Eric's eyes were cold, as was his expression, and he was at least twenty pounds thinner than Nick. There was also the attire.

Nick was all cowboy today in his jeans, white shirt and boots. Eric was wearing a dark-navy suit with a scarlet-red tie.

"What do you want?" Nick demanded.

Eric took a puff from his thin brown cigar. "You know, you should work on your social skills. Most people issue a polite greeting before they launch into a verbal attack."

"This isn't a social call. What do you want?" Nick repeated. But he didn't just repeat it. His voice lowered to a dangerous snarl.

"To have a morning chat with my little brother." Eric came closer and put out his arm as if to shove his way past Nick. That didn't happen. Nick held his ground and blocked him from entering.

"You can say whatever you came to say while standing on the porch," Nick insisted. "Because you're not coming inside."

With his cigar clutched in his fingers, Eric made a vague motion behind him. "It's November, and it's cold out here."

"Then talk fast."

The corner of Eric's mouth hitched. "I came to meet your lover."

Nick stiffened. "She's not available."

But as if he'd known all along that she was there, Eric casually took another drag of his cigar and snared her gaze in the mirror. Yes, she'd been right about his eyes. They were pure ice and evil. Kelly didn't let that coldness put her off, even though she had to dodge Cooper's efforts when he tried to grab her.

"You have something to say to me, Mr. Lattimer?" Kelly challenged.

Nick didn't let her get too close. Huffing and mumbling at her, he stepped in front of her, practically blocking her view of Eric.

"So, Nick's moved you in here with him," Eric commented. "It's a mistake, you know."

Kelly met his venomous gaze and slipped her arm around Nick's waist. It seemed a good time to give Eric a show of affection to substantiate their claim of being lovers.

"You came here to warn her about me?" Nick interrupted before she could say anything. "You've wasted your time. And ours."

Eric blocked the door with his foot when Nick tried to shut it. "I came here to try to figure out what's going on."

Nick stared at his brother's foot for a moment before he lifted his head and glared at the man. "Nothing is going on that concerns you."

Eric narrowed his eyes. Gone was the cocky, calm demeanor, and he became tense. "I'm not so certain of that."

"Your paranoia's showing again," Nick informed him.

The intensity skyrocketed. Eric pulled back his shoulders, and his nostrils actually flared. "You're the one who threatened to kill me. Now I want to know what's so damn important that would put you on the defensive."

"When it comes to you, I'm always on the defensive, Eric. You're just too self-absorbed to notice." With that, Nick kicked his brother's foot away, but Eric caught the door anyway, holding it open.

Eric looked directly into her eyes when he spoke. "If you two are keeping secrets from me, you'll regret it. My estate is worth well over a hundred million dollars. I'm not going to share that with anyone, especially with the likes of you."

"Is that a threat?" Kelly asked.

But Eric didn't get a chance to confirm it. Nick came out on the porch. Not slowly, either. He stormed out of the house, and grasped the lapels of Eric's black Italian coat. Nick slammed him against the exterior brick wall. The impact was so forceful that Eric sputtered out a cough and dropped his cigar.

Nick's maneuver had two armed men springing from the limo parked in front of the ranch house.

Nick ignored the hired guns and got right in Eric's face. "Don't make me kill you."

Despite the cough and the obviously ruffled composure, Eric smiled. "You won't. There are the promises we made to our mother not to do harm to one another—"

"A promise you would have already broken if you knew you could get away with murder," Nick interrupted.

"There is that," Eric conceded. "But then, the right opportunity hasn't arisen, yet. Murder isn't really murder if the police can't link your death back to me." He lowered his voice. "You know how this has to end, Nick. One of us will have to kill the other. Cain and Abel. Except I won't be the one to die."

"No one has to die if you stay away from me and the people important to me." And with that, Nick let go of his brother's jacket and aimed a warning glare at the men who were about to step onto his porch.

They froze.

"Leave," Nick ordered Eric. "And don't come back."

Nick stepped back into the foyer and slammed the door, but he didn't move. He stood there for several moments as if trying to keep a chokehold on his temper. Kelly figured she was about to get a tongue-lashing because she'd disobeyed his order to stay away from Eric.

She was right.

"What you did was very dangerous," Nick informed her.

"Everything I do is dangerous, thanks to your brother. I didn't want him to think I was afraid of him." Even though she was afraid. Not for herself. But for what that evil man could do to Joseph and William.

"Remember, you have other guests in the solarium," Cooper reminded Nick.

Nick cursed under his breath. "Have them go to my office. I'll be there in a few minutes." He then turned and faced Kelly. "This conversation isn't over. Go back to your suite or the nursery and stay there until Eric is off the grounds."

Well, that got her heart racing. "You actually think he'll come back?"

He turned and walked toward his office. "Anything's possible with Eric."

Chapter Eight

Nick watched Kelly to make sure she returned to the nursery. He hadn't wanted her to confront Eric, and he definitely didn't want her in his office when he spoke to his other visitors: Todd Burgess and Paula Barker. In some ways, an association with them was just as dangerous as the meeting they'd had with his brother.

Because both Todd and Paula were agents with the Justice Department.

And Nick was helping them.

It was bad enough that Kelly was now on his brother's radar. He didn't want her to have to deal with the Feds.

He found the two federal agents waiting impatiently in his office. Paula, a tall, athletically built brunette, was pacing with her arms folded over her chest. Nick had run a background check on her, and she was considered to be one of the best agents at the department. A whiz at martial arts, Paula had successfully defended herself against men twice her size.

Todd, rail thin and too pale, didn't look as if he could defend himself against anyone, but Nick knew he had all the qualifications to be an agent. He'd made rank early and was hungry and ambitious enough for success that he would do whatever it took to bring down the prize that the Justice Department desperately wanted.

Eric.

Todd was seated across from Nick's desk, drumming his fingers on the chair arm. His thin mouth was pursed. Of course, it usually was. Ditto for his rumpled mud-brown hair. Even though Nick had only known the man for a few short months, he'd learned that Todd was not a man who relaxed easily.

Todd had his gaze fastened to the security monitor on Nick's desk. Kelly was sitting on the floor playing with the babies. Since it seemed like a violation of her privacy and because it wasn't any of Todd's business, Nick reached over and clicked it off.

"Sorry I kept you," Nick explained. He stepped inside and shut the door. "Eric was here."

That got their attention. Paula stopped pacing, and Todd slowly got to his feet.

"My brother didn't say anything incriminating," Nick volunteered. "Just the usual threats. This time the threats included Kelly Manning."

There, he'd put her name out there because he figured Kelly was the real reason for this visit. He'd informed the Justice Department of the kidnapping attempt and that he was bringing Kelly and her son to the ranch.

"How much does Ms. Manning know about you and what you're doing for the Justice Department?" Paula asked.

"Nothing."

Todd nodded. "Keep it that way. The more people who know about our investigation, the higher the chances are that Eric will find out about it."

Nick had no intention of telling Kelly because, simply put, he was playing a very dangerous game, and he didn't want her involved in it.

"You could use your brother's visit to set up a meeting with him," Todd continued. "As usual, wear a recording device in case he says something we can use."

Well, it'd be a first if Eric did spill anything. Nick had been trying to get his brother to say something incriminating for nearly six months, and each time he'd struck out.

"I don't want to meet with Eric again until I've worked out some things with Kelly," Nick commented. "But I think I'm getting close to discovering something about my brother's criminal activities. I've been in contact with one of his former employees, and I think with a little encouragement, she'll be willing to talk to me."

"Good," Todd grumbled. "We need a break here. We need to put Eric behind bars." Todd paused. "What's the name of the employee?"

"I'd rather keep that to myself right now."

In fact, Nick preferred to keep *all* the details to himself. Rosalinda McMillan, Eric's former secretary, had visited the ranch just three days earlier, on the same day that Kelly had posed as a waitress and tried to sneak into the nursery. Rosalinda could be in grave danger if Eric learned that she'd already talked to Nick and had copies of some of Eric's files. So far, they hadn't produced anything, but neither Rosalinda nor Nick was giving up.

Paula stopped right in front of him. "If you're worried about leaks in the department—"

"I'm always worried about that," Nick admitted. "And I don't want to put this person at risk until I'm certain the risk is worth taking."

Paula nodded, eventually, but Nick could tell she didn't approve of his withholding information. "What *things* do you have to work out with Kelly?" Paula wanted to know.

Nick tossed her a glare. "Things I'd like to keep private a while longer."

Paula glared back.

"Having her here at the ranch is too risky," Todd

concluded. "I'll find another place for her to stay." He took out his cell phone.

Nick snagged the man's wrist. "I don't want another place for her. I want her here so I can keep an eye on her. Eric sees her as a threat, and I'm almost positive he was behind the kidnapping attempt."

Todd shook off his grip. "Kelly Manning will only be a distraction that you don't need."

"I'll determine what I do or don't need." Nick poured himself another cup of coffee. It was cold, but he didn't care. He drank it anyway. "Look, I agreed to help you find evidence to convict Eric of racketeering and murder, but I didn't agree to let you take over my life."

"We're trying to keep you alive," Todd countered. "If Eric were to find out that you're helping us—"

"I'd be dead," Nick interrupted. "But he's not going to find out. And I'm not going to hand over control of my life to you two or anyone else."

Todd mumbled something that Nick didn't want to hear. "Arrange to have another meeting with Eric. Use Kelly Manning to push some of his buttons."

Not a chance. He didn't want to give Eric any more reason to come after Kelly.

"Better yet, why don't you try to pin the kidnapping attempt on my brother?" Nick countered. "That would get him arrested."

"We've looked," Paula answered. "There isn't any

evidence to connect him. Or anyone else for that matter. The shell casing from the fired shot hasn't produced a match, and even though you had a scuffle with one of them, there was no recoverable DNA or trace from your clothing."

"Then dig deeper," Nick snarled. "I've got my own issues to deal with." He checked his watch. It was barely 10:00 a.m., and he was tired. Bone tired. Plus, he needed to check on William. Other than the video images, he hadn't seen him all morning. "You can show yourselves out."

It wasn't a request.

Nick followed them, intending to head to the nursery as soon as Paula and Todd were out of the house, but Cooper was outside the office door waiting for him.

"It's important," Cooper immediately said.

Nick stepped back inside his office. "It'd better be."

"My friend at the lab just called. As soon as I took in the vials, he ran a new test on the DNA."

Nick hadn't expected to hear anything so soon. And judging from Cooper's worried expression, Nick wasn't sure he wanted to hear it.

"The lab guy explained the test to me," Cooper continued. "But I couldn't make heads or tails of what he was talking about. Something to do with genetic markers. Anyway, he said the test is too new to hold up in court, but he assures me that it's almost as accurate as the old way."

When his lungs started to ache, Nick forced himself to breathe. "And?"

"And it verifies that you're Joseph Manning's biological father."

Nick groaned and leaned his back and head against the wall. There it was. The news Nick prayed he wouldn't hear. The news that would change his life forever.

But at the same time he was worried about the danger, every ounce of him filled with joy. And dread. He was a father. Joseph was indeed his precious little boy. But claiming him would be a fatal error.

"So, it looks as if there was a baby switch after all," Cooper concluded.

Yes. And he knew exactly why Meredith had arranged it. Later, much later, after he figured out how to deal with this, Nick also needed to learn how Meredith had done it. Had she hired someone? If so, that someone needed to be found and warned, so that he or she wouldn't talk to Eric. His brother couldn't learn about this.

"You'll tell no one about the DNA test," Nick insisted. "In fact, if Kelly asks, you'll lie to her. You'll tell her that there is no DNA match."

That lie was a necessity that just might keep his son alive. Like Meredith's lie. Nick certainly didn't blame his former lover for what she'd done. In fact, he was grateful. If she hadn't switched the boys, his son would be dead.

"The lab sheet should arrive sometime tomorrow," Cooper told him. "What should I do with it?"

Nick knew what had to be done. "Destroy any evidence of the DNA and make sure to clean up at the lab. This info dies right here in this room with us."

"Excuse me?" he heard someone say.

It was Kelly. She was standing in the doorway of his office.

And judging from her expression, she'd heard every word he said.

Chapter Nine

"Are the babies okay?" Nick immediately asked.

"They're fine."

Cooper mumbled something about having an appointment, and he headed out, leaving them alone to hash out what was apparently a problem.

Kelly hesitated, studying him and wondering what the heck to say. Unfortunately, she'd only heard enough to realize that Nick was about to cover up something to do with the DNA.

"I was about to go to the nursery to check on William," Nick added.

"No need to do that right now. Greta and I just finished giving both Joseph and him their baths, and she was going to read to them before putting them down for their morning naps."

He looked disappointed. "Thanks."

"You don't have to thank me," she insisted. "I love spending time with them. What I don't love is hearing things that make me wonder if I can really trust you."

Kelly had to hand it to Nick. He didn't issue one of his Lattimer orders and storm off so he could avoid this confrontation. He stood there, waiting for the inevitable questions. Kelly didn't make him wait long.

"What DNA results are Cooper and you going to destroy?" she asked.

He lifted his right shoulder, a gesture that made this all seem routine. "Everything that has anything to do with Joseph, William, you or me. I don't want Eric to get his hands on something that he can misinterpret."

Kelly gave that some thought. "So, you don't have the results back yet, you were just thinking ahead?"

He nodded.

That was it. No other information.

Was he telling her the truth? Kelly didn't know, and she considered pressing him to find out more. She was almost positive she'd interrupted a critical conversation. Still, it didn't matter. Soon, she'd have her own tests results. If and when they confirmed what she feared—that Nick was Joseph's biological father—Kelly would confront him then.

But heaven help him if he'd lied. Their situation was already bad enough without adding dishonesty to the mix.

"My husband lied to me," she heard herself say. She frowned and wanted to smack herself. Sheez.

What was wrong with her? "Sorry, that was too much information."

"What did he lie about?" Nick immediately asked.

"Everything important." She considered stopping but decided what the heck. Maybe if she told him, Nick would understand how important the truth was to her, even if the truth terrified her. "His job, for one thing. He was a cop and there were problems in the department. He told his superiors and got the reputation of being a snitch. He said it didn't matter, that he was working a desk job. He wasn't. And he was killed while on what was supposed to be a routine raid of a crack house."

"He might not have told you the truth because he was trying to protect you," Nick pointed out.

"About that, maybe. But at his funeral, his mistress showed up and caused a scene. Lots of shouts and accusations. She blamed me for Louis's death."

Because she suddenly needed something to do, Kelly walked to the massive black granite and glass fireplace and looked up at the painting above it. Not standard rancher decor. It was a black-and-white photograph of a crystal bowl overflowing with lemons.

"You didn't know your husband was having an affair before then?" Nick asked.

"Didn't have a clue." She tore her attention from the photograph. "And I lost it when I found out that it had been going on for over a year. Because I couldn't get up out of bed in the morning, I checked myself into the hospital. But then, you already knew that."

Nick made a concurring sound. "You had reason to lose it."

She heard the sympathy in his voice, and it felt better than it should have. Kelly pushed that good feeling aside. "Yes, I guess I did."

She turned, and their gazes met. The air was always so charged when they were around each other. It made her wonder if something real could have developed between them if they'd met under different circumstances.

"You're positive that Eric's not still out there lurking around?" she asked.

"Believe me, he and his entourage are long gone. I have security cameras all along the ranch road that leads to the highway."

Relieved, Kelly nodded. "That doesn't surprise me. If I had a brother like that, I'd be doing the same thing." She paused. "Did you really swear to your mother that you wouldn't kill Eric?"

"No. I told her I'd try not to harm him. That's it. No promises. My mother didn't push for more of a guarantee. She knew what Eric was."

That wasn't the scenario she'd built in her mind. "So, why did she leave everything to him?"

"Because she was afraid Eric would kill me. She

died when I was barely sixteen. Eric was already twenty-five and well-known for his cutthroat business practices. Our father had died of lung cancer shortly after I was born. So, my mother left the bulk of the estate to Eric. She excluded me from inheriting anything but the ranch and college tuition, but where she made a mistake was not excluding my heirs. If she had, we wouldn't be going through all of this."

True. And all because of a poorly worded will. It seemed unfair. But then, what Nick had dealt with for years was the ultimate unfairness.

"You weren't disappointed when your mother left you only this ranch?" she asked.

"No. I think I got a good deal."

Puzzled, Kelly scratched her eyebrow. "I read about the ranch before I came here. It was in shambles when you took control of it. By the time you were twenty-six, it was turning a massive profit."

And now that Nick was thirty-three, it wasn't just profitable, it was one of the most successful cattle ranches in the state. His success showed, too. Not just in the ranch itself but in the way he managed his life. Kelly supposed that some people would credit his business degree from Harvard for that, but his determination and fortitude obviously hadn't hurt, either.

He moved closer to her. So close that she took in his scent. Deodorant soap, a woodsy aftershave and the cream-laced coffee that he'd just drunk. His scent was manly and homey at the same time. But then, that was Nick. A man of contradictions.

"You have something on your mind," he said.

Definitely. But it wasn't just one thing. There were lots of things on her mind. Where to start? Oh, yes. Best to start with a good air clearing.

"I want to hate you," she admitted.

"Then hate me." He smiled.

Kelly frowned. "You know I don't. It's crazy. *I'm* crazy. But despite the fact that I don't totally trust you, I don't hate you."

Still standing side by side, he stared down at her. Oh, those eyes. Cool gray and sizzling hot. Another contradiction, like the man himself. She could feel the ache stir for him deep within her body. An ache that confused her and made her mad at herself.

How could she feel this way?

But she didn't have time to answer her own question.

Nick cursed. It was raw. "I don't want this to happen, either. Usually I have willpower when it comes to this sort of thing."

Kelly didn't doubt it. Heck, she had willpower in spades. One lover in her entire twenty-eight years of life. No one could have ever called her adventurous when it came to matters of the heart. But she seemed to have developed an adventurous streak when it came to Nick.

He gave her a searing look a split second before he lowered his head and kissed her.

His mouth was cool. A surprise. She'd thought the heat would be there, as well. But more than heat was the finesse. Nick was very good at kissing, she soon learned.

He buried one of his hands deep into her hair. The other hand went around the back of her neck so that he controlled the movement, the pace. But Kelly wasn't protesting. That kiss was everything she'd dreamed about and more.

He wasn't gentle. She doubted he could be. The intensity raged through them both and filled the room until everything seemed to be racing out of control.

Her breath. Her mind. Her heart.

He pushed her against the wall, rattling some nearby pictures. Neither of them cared. All that mattered was the kiss. It had to continue. Kelly coiled her arms around him and pulled him closer.

Body against body.

And in that moment Kelly knew this kiss could take her places that she shouldn't go.

NICK KNEW he'd lost his frickin' mind. He was kissing Kelly, something both knew they shouldn't be doing.

Did that stop him?

No.

Nor did he stop when he realized this was

turning into more than a kiss. Much more. He had Kelly pressed against the wall, and the kiss was hot, deep and long. It was obviously turning up the heat in both of them because they soon fought to make the kiss even deeper. To make the body contact even harder.

So, that's what they did.

Nick slid his hands down her arms, laced his fingers with hers and pressed the backs of her hands against the wall. Their bodies adjusted to the newly created space, and his pulse jumped when he felt her aroused nipples on his chest.

Kelly reacted to the contact. Her moan was deep and throaty and totally feminine, and the most erotic sound he'd ever heard.

Anxious to hear more, Nick took the kiss to her neck, to the place just below her right earlobe. She moaned again and arched her body into his so that her sex touched his. Nick was certain that his eyes crossed from the sheer pleasure of that intimate contact.

The little voice in the back of his head kept telling him to stop, but it was getting harder and harder to hear with his heartbeat drumming in his ears. Besides, Kelly obviously didn't want to stop, either. She used her entire body to caress him.

The kissing and the touching continued until it reached a frantic pace. Kelly fought to get her hands free, and when Nick released them, her arms went around him again. Nick hadn't thought they could get any closer, but it happened.

For a few seconds, anyway.

Until he heard the voice over the intercom.

"Mr. Lattimer, would you like some more coffee?" he heard Esther, the cook, ask.

He tore his mouth from Kelly's neck and took a moment to compose himself before pressing the button to respond. "No." Unfortunately, he had to clear his throat and repeat it so that his one-word response would have sound.

Blinking, Kelly stared at him. She looked well kissed and shell-shocked. Nick knew how he felt.

"Where did that come from?" she asked.

Nick moved away from her so that he wouldn't be tempted to go back for round two. Even if his body thought that another round with Kelly was an excellent idea.

"It was lust," he assured her. "Pure lust."

Her breath was still gusting, and she bobbed her head. "I don't remember lust ever feeling so…lustful."

"That's the trouble with lust. It can be deceptive. And dangerous, because it's also distracting. We don't need any distractions right now."

Another bob of her head. Kelly continued to lean against the wall. "That sounds very logical. I don't think logic stands much of a chance against lust, though."

"No," Nick agreed. And he wanted to kick himself for the way he felt. "We'll just have to be more cautious when we're around each other."

Heck, he wanted to kick himself for saying that, too, because being careful wouldn't make him stop wanting Kelly. His body knew it, and he knew it. What he needed was to continue his search to find incriminating evidence that would lead to Eric's arrest. He damn sure didn't need to be making out with Kelly against the wall of his office.

He heard the slight crackle of the intercom again. "I don't want any coffee," Nick told the cook.

"It's not about the coffee, sir," Esther said. "I was walking by the security monitor in Cooper's office, and I saw something. Two men are climbing the fence out in the east pasture. Are they supposed to be there?"

Nick did a quick mental inventory of the projects he had going on, and having two men in the east pasture wasn't on the agenda.

"Where's Cooper?" he asked. Nick hurried to his desk, pushed his cell phone and keys aside so he could reach the security keyboard. He pressed in the codes to send the images of the east pasture to the monitor.

"I don't know, sir. He's not at his desk."

Nick cursed when he heard her response and when he verified that there were indeed two men. They were dressed all in black, wearing bandannas over their throats and mouths, and both were armed.

"Lock down the place," Nick ordered the house-keeper. "Secure all the doors and windows. And send someone to find Cooper."

"What's going on?" Kelly asked. She hurried across the room and looked at the monitor. "My God. Are those the same two men who tried to kidnap Joseph and me?"

"Could be." And that meant these goons might try to do the same again.

They wouldn't succeed.

Nick took the monitor, switched it to battery backup and began to race down the hall toward the nursery. Kelly was right on his heels. Nick threw open the door and spotted the babies playing on the floor. Greta was reading a story to them.

The relief was instant. They were safe. For now. But Nick had to make sure it stayed that way.

"What's wrong, sir?" Greta asked.

"We have intruders on the grounds. Call the sheriff just in case the silent alarm didn't trigger when the men came over the fence, and then I want Kelly, you and the babies in the panic room."

Greta nodded. He saw terror in her eyes and in every inch of her body. "What are you going to do?"

"I need to go out there."

Kelly was already shaking her head before he finished. "It's too dangerous."

But she didn't have a say in this. He couldn't let

those gunmen get any closer to the house. If that happened, they could fire shots inside, and anyone—including the babies—could be hit.

"Lock the door when I leave," he instructed. "And stay in the panic room."

Nick ignored Kelly's protests and raced out to confront the enemy.

Chapter Ten

Kelly's hands were shaking as she locked the nursery door. Actually, she felt shaky all over, but she tried to contain her fear and concentrate on what had to be done.

"We need to call the sheriff," she said, and reached for the phone.

"I'll do it once we're out of here," Greta volunteered.

First, though, she opened the door to what Kelly thought was a walk-in closet. But it was no ordinary closet. There was another door concealed at the back of it. Greta pressed in a code on a keypad tucked in the corner, and the door opened. Kelly soon saw that there was a short set of stairs that led to what Nick had referred to as the panic room. An apt word, since Kelly felt like panicking.

Greta and she each scooped up a baby and hurried into the room. It was larger than the nursery and decorated in a similar style, but there were no windows, and the door that Greta used to shut them off from the rest of the house was metal. No doubt bulletproof.

"You can use that to keep an eye on Mr. Lattimer," Greta suggested, pointing to the security monitor on a table on the far side of the room. She put William on the floor to play, and Kelly did the same with Joseph.

Kelly didn't refuse Greta's offer. While the woman made the call to the sheriff, Kelly stepped around the babies, who began to play with some stuffed animals, and hurried to the monitor. She quickly figured out how to use the tiny keyboard to switch camera angles.

Kelly zeroed in on the intruders. Even though they had something covering the lower parts of their faces, she could see that one of them had dark hair. The other was at least a head taller and had a stocky build.

They were in a pasture dotted with huge round hay bales, and were slowly making their way straight for the house. She did a quick assessment of their location and realized they were on the opposite side from the nursery and panic room. That didn't mean they would stay there.

"The sheriff's on the way," Greta relayed.

Good. Unfortunately, they might need all the help they could get. But the question was—would the sheriff get there in time to stop something terrible from happening?

Kelly used the keyboard to bring up new camera angles, until she found Nick. He was by one of the many barns, slowly making his way toward the men.

Oh, God.

He was going for a showdown, even though he was outnumbered. And why? To protect them, of course. He was risking his life for them. Kelly didn't want to thank him for that. She wanted to throttle him. Why hadn't he just stayed inside the panic room with them until the sheriff arrived? She switched between the images of Nick and the gunmen until she finally figured out a way to put the images on a split screen.

"Greta," someone said from over the intercom. It was Esther. "I can't find Cooper."

"Keep looking," Kelly interrupted.

Though she had to wonder—where was Nick's security guru when they needed him most?

"Mr. Lattimer knows how to take care of himself," Greta said softly.

They were words meant to comfort her, no doubt. But Kelly wouldn't be comforted until Nick was back inside and safe.

"He shouldn't have gone out there alone," Kelly mumbled.

And then she saw something on the screen that caused her fears to shoot through the roof. The two men stopped, said something to each other and one motioned in the direction of the barn where Nick was.

Then the men split up.

"Mercy," Kelly said under her breath. "They know where Nick is."

"What?" Greta asked, hurrying to the monitor.

Kelly tapped the image of the man on the lower portion of the screen. "The dark-haired one is trying to sneak around so he can ambush Nick."

She didn't have to wait long to have her theory confirmed. The taller gunman stood and fired a shot at the barn.

Nick took cover behind the barn and aimed his weapon. He probably didn't know the fired shot had been a ploy to distract him so that the other man could sneak up behind him.

"I can't sit here and watch him die." Kelly got to her feet. "Is there anyway we can call Nick?"

"His cell phone."

"It's on his desk." She remembered him pushing it aside when he used the monitor. He hadn't taken it with him.

And that left Kelly with a huge decision.

Except it wasn't really a decision. Nick had already saved her from the kidnappers once. Now, she had to do something to save him.

"Is there an extra gun in the house?" Kelly asked—though she already knew the answer. With Nick's concern about safety, there were probably plenty of firearms around.

Greta's blue eyes widened, but she didn't seem shocked by the question or by what Kelly intended to do.

The nanny went to a cherub painting on the wall and lifted it. Beneath it was a safe. She hurriedly opened it and extracted a Glock.

"You know how to use this?" Greta asked, handing her the gun and the magazine of ammunition.

Kelly nodded. "My late husband was a cop. He taught me how to shoot."

But Kelly had never thought she would have to use that particular skill.

"When the sheriff arrives, let him know what's going on," Kelly instructed. She went to the babies, leaned down and kissed both of them.

She didn't linger. Didn't waste any time. Because Nick's life hung in the balance.

"Be careful," she heard Greta say.

Joseph babbled bye-bye and William echoed it, the sounds nearly breaking Kelly's heart. She wanted to stay with the babies, to make sure they were safe, but right now the only one in real danger was Nick.

Kelly left the panic room, went into the kitchen and found the cook and the head ranch hand, a lanky cowboy with weathered skin and a battered Stetson. He was seventy if he was a day. He introduced himself as Zeke and immediately tried to talk her out of leaving the house.

She didn't listen.

However, Kelly did inform him of her plan. She'd get as close to the barn as possible so she could alert Nick and keep an eye out for the dark-haired gunman who was trying to sneak up behind him.

She opened the back door cautiously, and looked out to see if she could spot the men. Neither was in her line of sight, but that didn't stop her. Kelly eased down the porch steps, into the backyard and raced toward a hedge. She hid behind it, probably using the same route that Nick had and made it to the edge of the barn.

No sign of Nick.

Or the second gunman.

She stopped and listened for footsteps, but all she could hear was the brutal November wind assaulting her. Kelly ignored the cold and the goose bumps riffling over her skin, quietly went to the front edge of the barn, and peeked around the corner.

There was suddenly a gun right in her face.

She choked back a shriek and had already geared up for a fight for her life before her brain registered that the person on the other end of the gun was Nick.

"What the hell are you doing out here?" he whispered in a snarl.

It took her several moments to find enough breath to speak. "One of the gunmen is about to ambush you."

The words had no sooner left her mouth than she

saw movement at the corner of the barn behind Nick. It was the dark-haired gunman.

And he took aim.

Nick must have sensed what was happening because he tackled her and sent them both plummeting to the ground. The fall was cold and hard, and Kelly felt pain shoot through her. Nick didn't waste any time. With his body covering hers, he turned, aimed and fired.

Just as the gunman shot at them.

The bullet clipped off a chunk of the barn.

Nick and Kelly were out of position to return fire, but Nick quickly remedied that. He rolled off her, and in the same motion, he spun around and took aim.

But it was already too late.

The gunman wasn't there.

She caught just a glimpse of him running across the pasture.

Nick sprang from the ground and went in pursuit. Kelly shouted for him to be careful, but she doubted he heard her. His attention was totally focused on the gunman. Correction. The gun*men*. When she raced to the end of the barn, Kelly spotted both of them.

The dark-haired man was hightailing it out of there, but the taller one was still in the pasture, and he took aim at Nick.

Nick fired at him first, and the shot slammed into the gunman's weapon. Sparks flew, literally, and some must have caught the tall guy in the right eye because his hand went in that direction.

"Put down your gun!" Nick shouted to him.

The gunman didn't. Instead, he darted behind a massive bale of hay, and Kelly caught a glimpse of him running away in the same direction as his comrade.

Nick began to run, as well. He used the hay bales and the fence for cover. The men were so far ahead of him that it was almost impossible for him to catch up with them. And if he did, what then?

Kelly didn't want to think about that.

Using the same cover that Nick had, she followed in his footsteps in case it did come down to a gun fight. She couldn't stand by and just watch him get hurt. Or worse.

But the gunmen no longer seemed interested in a confrontation. They didn't even look back. They just continued to run until they barreled over the fence and disappeared into the dense woods on the other side.

And that left Kelly with one burning question. Why had they given up so easily?

Maybe because they hadn't expected anyone to return fire? But that didn't make sense. On a Texas ranch there was a solid chance that someone would have a weapon and know how to use it. So maybe the men had come for a quick in-and-out kidnapping and had gotten scared when that didn't happen? It was a question that she was certain Nick would want answered ASAP.

Nick didn't turn and come back as she figured he would. He sprinted right over the fence after those men.

NICK WAS SEVERAL STEPS past being furious. These SOBs had come onto his property, shot at Kelly and him and had planned to do God knows what. He wanted to find them and beat answers out of both of them.

But he stopped and thought of Kelly and the babies.

Running in a thick forest after two armed men wasn't the brightest thing he could do. In fact, the men might be out there waiting to ambush him. If that happened, they might be able to gain access to the house. Or they might just grab Kelly and run.

Nick glanced behind him and confirmed that Kelly was still standing there.

Cursing and feeling totally useless that he couldn't end this threat here and now, Nick turned around and raced toward her. She levered up and aimed her gun. She was watching his back. Nick was thankful for it, but he hated that she had to put herself in a situation like this. He'd lived with danger most of his life, but this wasn't something Kelly should have to experience.

"Are you okay?" Kelly asked the moment he got to her.

He didn't take the time to answer. Nick didn't

84

she'd thought she was fine. It took Daniel's words and Brooke's question to make her realize she was far from a full recovery.

She'd made a start with her sister's help and she intended to go forward now. Sarah felt as if she'd been living in a darkened room and some-one had suddenly opened a door, letting in the fresh air and sunshine. She could feel its warmth slowly seeping into the coldest part of her. The feeling was liberating. She realized it was only a small step and she had a long way to go, but she was ready to face life again with Serena and her family behind her.

All too soon, they were saying goodbye and Sarah experienced a moment of sadness for all he years she and Serena had missed. But they ad each other now and th t's what

She held

The Harlequin Reader Service® — Here's How it Works:

Accepting your 2 free Harlequin Intrigue® larger print books and 2 free gifts places you under no obligation to buy anything. You may keep the books and gifts and return the shipping statement marked "cancel." If you do not cancel, about a month later we'll send you 6 additional Harlequin Intrigue® larger print books and bill you just $4.49 each in the U.S. or $5.24 each in Canada, plus 25¢ shipping & handling per book and applicable taxes if any.* That's the complete price and – compared to cover prices of $5.25 each in the U.S. and $6.25 each in Canada – it's quite a bargain! You may cancel at any time, but if you choose to continue, every month we'll send you 6 more books, which you may either purchase at the discount price or return to us and cancel your subscription.

*Terms and prices subject to change without notice. Sales tax applicable in N.Y. Canadian residents will be charged applicable provincial taxes and GST. Offer limited to one per household. All orders subject to approval. Books received may vary. Credit or debit balances in a customer's account(s) may be offset by any other outstanding balance owed by or to the customer. Please allow 4 to 6 weeks for delivery.

If offer card is missing write to:
Harlequin Reader Service, 3010 Walden Ave., P.O. Box 1867, Buffalo, NY 14240-1867

BUSINESS REPLY MAIL
FIRST-CLASS MAIL   PERMIT NO. 717-003   BUFFALO, NY

POSTAGE WILL BE PAID BY ADDRESSEE

HARLEQUIN READER SERVICE
3010 WALDEN AVE
PO BOX 1867
BUFFALO NY 14240-9952

NO POSTAGE
NECESSARY
IF MAILED
IN THE
UNITED STATES

want her out in the open a second longer. She'd already had more than enough risks.

Nick caught her arm to get her moving, and they ran back into the house. Esther was there. Alarmed, of course. And she'd apparently called his head ranch hand because Zeke Dixon was there as well.

"What do you need me to do?" Zeke immediately asked. Nick trusted Zeke who'd been with him the entire time he'd owned the ranch.

"There's plenty to do," Nick answered. "First things first—did anyone find Cooper?"

Both Zeke and Esther shook their heads. Nick cursed again. Here, there'd been a major breach in security and his security manager wasn't around— again. The same thing had happened the night Kelly came to the ranch and tried to sneak into the nursery.

"Zeke, when Sheriff Cross gets here, explain to him what's going on. Have him send some deputies to search those woods." Nick put his weapon back into his slide holster. "Esther, I need you to call Rosalinda McMillan, Eric's former secretary. You'll find her name in my Rolodex in my office. Ask her to come to the ranch immediately. I need to talk to her."

"What does Eric's former secretary have to do with this?" Kelly asked when Zeke and Esther hurried out to do what he'd asked of them.

"I need her to tell me everything she knows about Eric so that maybe I can get him arrested." He left out the part about his working for the feds. For now. "That's the only way these attacks are going to stop."

Nick headed toward Cooper's office, and Kelly was right behind him.

"What if she's still loyal to Eric?" Kelly asked.

"I've considered that she might be stringing me along so she can report back to Eric that I'm out to get him. But Eric already knows I'd do just about anything to put him away, so she wouldn't exactly be telling him anything new."

But Nick hoped that Rosalinda was on the up and up. He desperately needed something.

They went by the panic room on the way to Cooper's office, but Nick could hear cries before they even opened the door. The cries belonged to not one baby, but both. The nanny was trying to rock them, but they were obviously not happy.

Nick scooped up William, kissed him and the baby hushed immediately.

"I think they sense that's something's wrong," Greta commented.

"No doubt," Kelly said. She traded Greta her gun for Joseph. The little boy's cries tapered off.

Nick decided it was a good idea for the babies to be with them anyway, so he hitched his shoulder toward the door. "I need to check something in Cooper's office."

Kelly nodded, held Joseph snugly against her and

followed him. When they made it to Cooper's office, Nick sat at the desk and started going through the surveillance images of the past half hour. He stopped when the saw the file open on Cooper's computer.

"Denny Russell," Nick read aloud.

"What about him?" But Kelly didn't wait for an answer. She went behind the desk with Nick and looked at the screen.

Nick quickly read through Cooper's notes and found something he certainly hadn't known about. A vehicle registered to P.I. Denny Russell had been spotted at the locked front entrance gate to the ranch just the night before. According to Cooper's evaluation of the surveillance tapes, Denny had actually gotten out of his car and tried to climb the fence before the alarm sounded. Then he'd gotten back into his vehicle and driven off.

"What would Denny Russell have been doing here at the ranch?" Nick asked her.

She shrugged. "Maybe checking on me. But he didn't say anything about driving out here."

It wasn't unreasonable that a friend would want to keep an eye on Kelly. But what bothered Nick was the secretive way he'd gone about it. "Do you trust him?"

"Of course," she said without hesitation. "He was my husband's former partner and friend. He's helped me out a lot since Louis's death. Besides, if you're thinking Denny's behind these kidnapping attempts, he has no reason to do that to me."

"Oh, he had a reason," Nick concluded. "He might kidnap you to keep you away from me."

She opened her mouth, probably to protest that, but she slowly closed it. "Eric is our suspect. Not Denny."

"But Eric's not working alone. Someone is helping him."

"What about Cooper?" she fired back. "Do you trust him?"

"Not anymore," Nick admitted. He shifted a squirming William so he could do a computer search of Cooper's recent files.

Kelly kissed Joseph's cheek and began to rock him. "And then there's Paula and Todd, the visitors who were here just a little while ago."

Nick stared at her. "You think those two bandanna-wearing gunmen were Paula and Todd?"

"I just don't know. Do you trust them?" Kelly countered.

Nick debated how much he should tell her, and he decided she needed to hear this. Especially since it might be *this* that had precipitated the attacks.

He got up and shut the door. "Paula and Todd are Justice Department agents. And I'm helping them find evidence that they can use against Eric."

Judging from the way she sucked in her breath, she hadn't expected him to admit that. "How long has this been going on?"

"Weeks. But things escalated the night of the

party. The night you were here. Eric's former secretary, Rosalinda, showed up and told me that she would help me find solid proof that I could use to have Eric arrested."

"And you believed her?"

"Yes. Eric's also her former lover. He dumped her for another woman. I think she'd do just about anything to get back at him."

Kelly shook her head. "And Eric might be willing to do anything to stop her. Do you think he found out she'd visited you?"

"Maybe. I try to keep security tight here, but after what happened today, I wonder if I have any security at all." That would change. By the end of the day, he'd have a complete overhaul of the system.

That would likely include a new security manager.

"Who knows that you're helping the Justice Department?" Kelly asked.

"Paula, Todd, their boss, you and me. Needless to say, I don't want anyone else to find out."

The phone buzzed, and Nick shifted William again so he could hit the speaker function.

"Rosalinda McMillan will be here in a few minutes," Esther informed him. "She was already on her way to the ranch to talk to you. Sheriff Cross is here, as well. He wants to speak to both of you."

"Send him to my office," Nick instructed. Hopefully, he'd be done with the sheriff before Rosalinda arrived.

"I will. One more thing—Ms. Manning has a call from Denny Russell on line two."

Nick looked at her, to see what she wanted to do. Kelly didn't eagerly grab the phone. In fact, she hesitated. Then she finally reached over and pressed the button for line two.

"Denny," she greeted.

"I tried your cell phone, but you've turned it off. Is everything okay?"

She groaned softly and rubbed her hand over her face. "It's not a good time to talk."

"Well, you'll want to hear this. I just got back the first set of preliminary test results, and you were right. You're William's mother."

Chapter Eleven

There it was. The truth. The DNA test had only proven what Kelly had felt deep within her soul.

William was her baby.

Her heart filled with love and joy, but her stomach sank with loss and grief. She'd lost the first year with her baby, but if she'd had that year, she wouldn't have become Joseph's mother.

And she *was* his mother.

He was as much her son as William was, she thought as she disconnected the call.

"I'll give you some time," Nick said, standing. "Besides, I need to talk to the sheriff."

Kelly needed to do the same. At the least, she'd have to give a statement. Heaven knew how long that would take. She didn't want to spend one moment with the sheriff. She wanted to hold her babies and sit down with Nick so they could come to terms with what they'd just learned.

"William will always be my son," he mumbled and headed for the door.

Greta was there, waiting, and she took William from him. The woman's gaze met Kelly's. "I'll watch them both while you talk to the sheriff," she offered.

Kelly nodded, followed her to the nursery and deposited Joseph on the floor so he could play. Greta did the same with William. The two boys played together happily. Side by side.

Her babies.

One brief glance at Nick, though, and Kelly knew it would be a huge fight to claim her biological son. And Kelly wasn't even sure she had the right to do that. Nick was the only father William had known. He'd been a good father, too. Did she have a right to try to take William away from him? Perhaps not. But that wouldn't stop her. She couldn't imagine a life without a child she'd carried and given birth to, just as she couldn't imagine a life without Joseph.

Nick didn't say a word as they made their way to his office. But he broke his silence to introduce Kelly to Sheriff Clayton Cross. He wasn't exactly what Kelly had been expecting. With a name like his, she'd thought the small-town Texas sheriff would be more of a cowboy. He wasn't. He wore khakis, shoes, not boots, and there wasn't a Stetson in sight.

"Nick, Ms. Manning," he greeted. "I suspect

you're both upset, maybe even in shock right now. Are either of you hurt?"

Kelly shook her head, hoping Sheriff Cross didn't expect her to speak. In the past hour someone had tried to kill her and she'd learned that William was her child. She was well past simply being upset.

"My deputies are checking out the area now," the sheriff continued. "I'm going to join them after I'm done here. We might get lucky and find some evidence that can help us identify these guys. While I'm going over the grounds with them, I'd like both of you to write down an account of what happened. I'll read them, and if I have any questions, I can call you later today."

"Thanks." Nick shook the man's hand, and the sheriff made a quick exit.

Kelly considered his exit a gift. Nick and she had to talk about what Denny had told her. But she didn't get a chance to even start the conversation because she heard the voice over the intercom.

"Rosalinda McMillan is here," Esther said. "She wouldn't wait in the sitting room as I asked her to do. She's on the way back to your office. And she doesn't seem to be in a very good mood."

"Great," Nick mumbled.

"There's more," the housekeeper continued. "Cooper called. He said he has an important meeting and he won't be back until morning."

This time Kelly mumbled, "Great." Just when they needed him most, the security guy wasn't around.

There was a knock at the door.

Kelly groaned softly and sank down into the chair across from his desk.

"This won't be a long visit," Nick promised her.

Good. Even though Kelly knew this meeting would be important, so was the conversation that she needed to have with Nick.

He opened the door, and a tall, leggy brunette came rushing into the room. The housekeeper was right. Rosalinda McMillan was not in a good mood. Her eyes were red and swollen, and she looked as if she'd just had a long cry.

"Eric has someone following me," she announced. Then her attention landed on Kelly. She became even more agitated. "Who is that?"

"Kelly Manning," Nick introduced, lifting his hand in her direction. "She wants Eric behind bars, too, so anything you can say to me, you can say to her."

"Really?" There was skepticism and distrust in Rosalinda's body language and tone.

Kelly nodded and made direct eye contact with the woman. "I believe Eric wants me dead."

Rosalinda shrugged. "And that's the reason I should just trust you?"

"No. You should trust me because we both want and need the same thing—to stop Eric. If we don't, he's going to hurt a lot of people. He's not only put Nick's and my life in danger, he's endangered my baby." Kelly waited until she saw the resignation and maybe even a little empathy in Rosalinda's expression. "You said that Eric had someone following you. Did the person follow you here, as well?"

"No. But I've been driving around for the past hour, just so I could lose the guy." Rosalinda touched a rumpled tissue to her nose. "I think Eric knows that I'm looking for evidence against him. And he's put some kind of eavesdropping equipment in my car and house. I can't find any bugs—I've looked—but I'm positive they're there. That's why I didn't want to tell you this on the phone."

Nick gave a heavy sigh. "What makes you think all of this?"

"Eric called me," she explained. "He didn't come out and say that he knew I was looking for evidence, but he made references to some casual phone conversations I'd had with friends. Then he threatened me. He reminded me of a confidentiality agreement I'd signed when I went to work for him. He said if I talked to anyone, that he would sue me or something. *Or something,*" Rosalinda repeated. "You and I both know what that *something* is."

"Then, it's too dangerous for you to continue to help me," Nick insisted.

Kelly added her own mental sigh of frustration.

That wasn't what they wanted to hear, but she knew why he'd told Rosalinda McMillan that. Eric would kill her if he found out she was betraying him, and neither Nick nor Kelly wanted this woman's death on their hands.

"I need some kind of protection from Eric," Rosalinda continued.

Nick nodded. Just a nod. And with that same heavy look on his face, he called someone he didn't identify by name and asked the person to come to the ranch to assist with witness protection for Rosalinda.

Because Kelly was watching him so closely, she saw his body language change. His jaw muscles tightened. He didn't say anything to the person on the other end of the line, but Kelly was positive he'd just heard more bad news.

"Thank you for arranging that," Rosalinda said when he finished the call. She obviously hadn't picked up on Nick's body language.

Nick waited a moment, as if trying to shake off the effects of that call. "Someone shot at Kelly and me a little while ago. By any chance, do you know anything about that?"

Rosalinda frantically shook her head. "No. Why would you think I did?"

"Just covering all bases," Nick assured her.

"It was Eric's men who tried to kill you, wasn't it?" she asked.

"Probably. But I don't have any proof."

She flattened her hand on her chest. "God, what have we gotten ourselves in to?"

"You'll be fine," Nick promised.

Kelly wondered if that was true. Had Nick learned something about the shooting from the caller?

"But you won't," Rosalinda concluded. "Eric despises you. He'll look for any excuse to come after you and kill you."

Because Nick didn't respond to that, Kelly stood and took the lead. "If you think of anything we can use against Eric, please call Nick."

Rosalinda nodded, and the tears started again.

"Why don't you wait in the sitting room?" Nick suggested. "The people who'll be handling your protection will be here soon, and Kelly and I have to do incident reports for the sheriff."

"Of course," she said, her voice trembling as she walked out.

Nick shut the door, leaned against it and cursed like a sailor.

"This has been a hell of a day," he grumbled.

"And it's not over," she reminded him.

He looked at her, and a thousand things passed between them unsaid but fully understood.

"The incident reports can wait," Kelly whispered. "So can whatever you just learned from that phone call. We need to address what Denny told us."

He pulled in a long breath, walked back to his desk and sat on the edge it, directly across from her so that their legs were practically touching. Kelly didn't let the physical contact cloud her mind. This was too important.

"Before you say anything," she started. "I think you should know that I sent both William's and your DNA to the lab to be tested."

She watched his intense gray eyes as that registered. "The water glass I used in your kitchen. You sent it to the lab."

She nodded.

"Hell."

That was it. His only verbal reaction. But they both knew that she would soon know the full truth.

"Well?" she prompted.

He reached out and slid his hand over hers. "We're past the point of lies. But in this case, the truth isn't going to set us free." He paused. "It's true."

Kelly's heart began to race out of control. "What's true?" She didn't want to assume anything here. She wanted it all spelled out.

"Everything you suspected. William is your son. And Joseph is mine."

She didn't have time to react to that because Nick continued.

"There's more. The Justice Department found out that someone hacked into the computer files of the lab you used about two hours ago and copied all the results of the DNA tests."

Each word felt like a fist pounding against her heart. "Oh, God."

"Yeah," Nick whispered. "Oh, God."

MORE THAN THE NUMBNESS and the bone-deep exhaustion, the number-one thing Nick felt was fear. Hell, it was hard for him to admit that, even to himself. He'd spent his life trying to be fearless. But this wasn't fear for himself.

This was fear for Kelly and their sons.

Because Nick knew that once Eric had proof of Joseph's paternity, he wouldn't just go after the child, Eric would go after all of them.

He glanced at Kelly, who was staring at her dinner plate. Actually, she was pushing food around with her fork. "You should eat," he reminded her.

She glanced at his own full plate—a perfectly grilled medium-rare t-bone, baked potato and spinach salad—and lifted her eyebrow.

"I'm not hungry, either," Nick said.

She stood, tossed her napkin onto the table. "I'm going to check on the boys."

Fatigue and worry was apparent throughout her entire body. Especially her eyes. But then, it'd been the day from hell.

Nick stood, too, tossing his napkin next to hers,

and followed Kelly to the nursery. She opened the door slowly and peeked inside. Both boys were sleeping in their cribs, which had been moved practically side by side. Greta wasn't with them, but he knew she was no doubt within earshot of the baby monitor. The woman believed in being on the job twenty-four/seven.

"I want to stay in here with them for a while," Kelly whispered.

Nick nodded, went to the monitor and let Greta know that Kelly and he would do baby duty for a while. He clicked off the device so they'd have some privacy.

"I'm waiting for you to yell at me," Nick said, keeping his voice low so that it wouldn't wake up the babies. "After all, I did lie to you about the DNA results."

Kelly sat on the floor, her back against the wall. "This lie is acceptable. You did it for all the right reasons. To protect us."

Surprised and pleased that there wouldn't be an argument and that they might get some down time, Nick sat next to her. She didn't object and didn't give him an uncomfortable look when his arm brushed against hers. In fact, she leaned against him, putting her head on his shoulder.

"You have a generous attitude about my lie," Nick told her.

"*Generous?* Right. I won't mention all the unkind

thoughts I had when I realized you hadn't told me the truth."

He frowned. "How unkind?"

"You don't want to know." She paused, glanced at him.

That glance and slight turn of her head put them even closer. Practically breath to breath. Nick didn't move away.

"Once I got past the unkind thoughts, I remembered something important," she continued. Her voice was silky now, and she didn't take her gaze from his. "You've been a good father to my son. I've been a good mother to yours."

He couldn't disagree with that. "You've been a fantastic mother."

She blushed and fought back a smile. Then she shrugged. "Of course, despite all this good parenthood talk, we've already said we aren't going to give up the child we've raised. That leaves us…where?"

"Between a rock and a hard place," Nick grumbled.

She chuckled, but it was laced with fatigue. "So many questions and no answers. We're dealing with custody issues, Eric and lots of people we can't trust."

Among other things.

Nick leaned over and kissed her. It wasn't long. Just a few seconds. Just enough time to give her a physical reminder of their biggest obstacle.

"Oh, and the lust," Kelly added. Her voice wasn't

just silky, it was hot liquid. "We're dealing with that, too."

Nick liked the sound of her voice, and he liked the flush of arousal on her cheeks.

"You'd forgotten about it?" he accused. Nick ran his tongue over his bottom lip and had the pleasure of tasting her there.

"Hardly. I can't get my mind off you."

Nick stared at her. "You're admitting that?"

"Why not? I've blabbered about everything else including my lack of sexual experience."

She had at that, and during that particular conversation, she'd mentioned something that'd snagged his interest. "You said your husband was the only man you'd slept with. Why?"

"Well, since his death, there just hasn't been time or anyone I wanted to be with."

"I can understand that, but you're an attractive woman. What about before you met your husband?"

"Before," she repeated, "I didn't have many good role models in my family for solid relationships, so I came up with my own rules."

"Rules?" And his mind was racing with all sorts of possibilities.

"Not naughty rules," she clarified, obviously noticing his expression. "I decided I wouldn't get serious with a man until I'd met his family and had celebrated a one-year anniversary with him. I got close a few times, but I held out, waiting for that anniversary celebration. I figured if I waited, then I'd really know this guy and that I wouldn't make the same mistakes as the rest of my family."

"But from what you've told me, in some ways your marriage was a mistake," he pointed out.

"It was in a lot of ways. I didn't wait for the anniversary celebration with Louis. I should have." She made a small sound of dismissal. "But then, I got William. I'd repeat those mistakes a thousand times over just to get him."

Nick felt the same way about Joseph.

She turned toward him, her jeans whispering against the carpet. "What about you? What are your rules for a relationship?"

The question didn't stick in his mind right away because the shift in posture made her blouse gape a bit, and Nick could see her extremely low-cut bra.

"Rules for relationship?" he repeated. "Cowboys don't really have those kind of rules. It clashes with our otherwise manly images."

He winked at her.

"No rules whatsoever?" Her mouth quivered as if she were fighting back a smile.

"Well, other than a drunk woman is off-limits and no playing around with friends' exes." He couldn't resist. Nick slipped his index finger under her neckline and traced the top of her breast. She moaned her pleasure. "But I suppose it wouldn't be smart for a rancher to get involved with a woman who was afraid of cows or horses. So, I guess that's a rule."

She stiffened slightly. "I'm afraid of horses."

Nick pulled back a little so he could study her face to see if she was joking or telling the truth. "Really?"

She nodded. "When I was a kid, I was riding a horse at my cousin's farm, and it threw me. Broke my arm. Horses are definitely not in my comfort zone." Her forehead bunched up. "So, does that mean you can't have a relationship with me?"

"It means," he said, pausing. "We might have to rethink our rules."

She smiled, and man, what a smile it was. It lit up her whole face, and Nick suddenly wanted nothing more than to taste that smile. To taste her.

So he did.

He lowered his head, put his mouth to hers and took everything that he wanted from her. Well, maybe not *everything*. But he knew a kiss would have to do.

She tasted better than her smile looked. And that was saying something. Nick savored that taste. It went through him like expensive whiskey. It must have had a similar effect on Kelly because she moved closer and closer until she was right up against him.

Even though the French kisses had ignited that roaring blaze inside them, everything seemed to slow down. The air became hot and thick. His pulse thudded to an easy rhythm that seemed as old as time. It was as if this kiss could go on forever.

Kelly broke away, gasping for breath. But as soon as she had recovered, she went back for more.

Nick slid his hands around her back, mainly so he wouldn't be tempted to start taking off her clothes. Kelly's palms went against his chest, adding just a small amount of space between them. Just enough so that her breasts weren't touching his chest. And the kisses continued.

Mercy, did they ever continue.

They made love to each other with their mouths until the heat began to create an urgency inside him. That was the problem with a good kissing session. If it was done right—and they were definitely doing it right—then the body eventually began to clamor for more.

Kelly shifted slightly, lowering her hands from his chest to his hips, and leaned forward. Nick did, too. It wasn't a good idea since they were trying to hold back, but he didn't even try to stop himself.

Then he did something totally stupid.

He pulled Kelly into his lap. And she went willingly.

There it was. The body-to-body fit that he knew he should have avoided. Because when Kelly landed in his lap, her sex also landed right against his erection. A perfect fit.

Nick went from feeling flames to being engulfed by an inferno. He sucked in his breath and grunted, which she seemed to take as an invitation to do more.

She turned, moving her legs until they straddled his hips.

"This won't go anywhere," she said.

Yeah, right. Other than seeing massive stars and having his heartbeat deafen him, his body was starting to veto his brain, and his erection was already begging for him to strip off her jeans and take her right there. To hell with the consequences.

"You're a great kisser," she whispered.

Nick's mind was a cloudy mess of raunchy thoughts. "Ditto. But you give a pretty darn good lap dance, too."

She pulled back slightly and smiled. Not an embarrassed smile, either. It was as naughty and raunchy as the thoughts racing through his head.

Though there were two layers of jeans and underwear separating them, Kelly did a nice little slippery slide that made him believe that clothes were not a barrier. He wasn't fast enough to stop her from doing it a second time.

His eyes crossed. He was ready to beg for mercy. And that's why he caught her hips to stop her from more of the sweet torture.

They sat there pressed against each other. Man, he wanted her bad. He wanted to unzip her, peel off those jeans, slide into the welcoming heat of her body and move hard and deep inside her.

"Does this mean we're quitting?" Her breath was fast and uneven, and she didn't sound as if she wanted to stop.

But Nick knew they couldn't continue. Even through the thick haze of passion, he was aware of that.

He wanted to suggest that they go elsewhere, but as hungry for her as he was—and he was hungry—Nick knew that dragging her off to bed wasn't a great idea. After all, just that morning gunmen had gotten onto the ranch. They had a deputy standing guard, but it probably wasn't a good idea to leave the babies alone.

Especially since Eric was going to come after Joseph.

That was all he needed, in order to accept that nothing sexually satisfying was going to happen tonight. He wouldn't rule out future nights, though. In fact, he was certain that he wouldn't be able to keep his hands off Kelly much longer. Judging from the sexually charged look she was giving him, she obviously felt the same.

"We're quitting," he mumbled, cursing with frustration.

Kelly groaned. She brushed a kiss on his mouth and moved off him, and he felt the loss immediately. She'd felt damn good against him, and he couldn't help but wonder just how much better it could get.

He didn't want to know. Not now anyway. Now he needed to get his body and mind off Kelly and her extremely effective lap dance.

Nick forced himself to move. He locked the nursery door and grabbed some of the floor pillows and an extra crib blanket.

"Get some sleep," he insisted.

He got down next to her, pulled her against him so they were spooning. Definitely not face-to-face. He didn't need to be tempted to kiss her again. Kelly settled against him, and he prayed she would indeed get some sleep.

Nick wouldn't. Not a chance.

As Kelly drifted off, he silently checked the slide holster in the back of his jeans to make sure his gun would be easy to get to if he needed it.

Chapter Twelve

When Nick heard the soft creak, he snapped to a sitting position and went for his gun. Thankfully, he didn't actually draw the weapon before he realized what made that sound.

It was Joseph.

He'd pulled himself up in the crib, and while he gripped the railing, his alert gaze landed on Nick.

Joseph grinned.

Nick was almost positive that he grinned back. Though he couldn't be sure of what he was doing. His heart kicked into overdrive, and it felt too big for his chest.

Kelly got up as well, probably because Nick's reach for his gun had startled her, but she soon smiled when she realized what was going on.

"Good morning, sweetheart," she greeted. Kelly stood, gently took Joseph from the crib and brought him onto the floor with them.

Joseph immediately climbed out of her arms and toddled toward Nick. Nick soon figured out why. Joseph was interested in his watch. He wasn't quiet about it, either. He babbled and tugged at the band, which woke William, who stood and began to clamor to get out of his crib. Kelly obliged, and Nick watched the magic happen when she took him in her arms.

Kelly drew William to her chest for a long hug.

Nick wanted to hang on to the priceless moment. Kelly holding William, Joseph in his lap. But unfortunately it only lasted a few seconds before there was a tap at the door. Nick reluctantly got up and unlocked it and faced Greta.

"Sorry to bother you, sir," she said peeking in at them. "But you have visitors."

Nick checked his watch. It was barely 8:00 a.m. "Who is it?"

"Paula Barker and Todd Burgess," Greta supplied. "Ms. Barker phoned about a half hour ago and said she wanted to see you this morning. I told her you were sleeping in and that I didn't want to disturb you just yet. Guess I didn't make it clear enough about the non-disturbing part, because she and Mr. Burgess showed up anyway. I have them in the sitting room. They say they must speak to you right away."

Nick groaned. What the heck did they want this time of morning? Whatever it was, it couldn't be good.

Greta's gaze landed on Kelly. "*You* have a visitor,

as well. Mr. Denny Russell. He said he's a close friend of yours, so I let him in."

That instantly alarmed Nick. "Russell's in the house?" he asked.

Greta nodded. "In your office."

Nick wanted to kick himself. He should have instructed his staff not to allow Denny Russell anywhere on the grounds and especially not inside the house. Not until he had the full background check he'd requested on the man that was likely waiting in Cooper's office. Nick would get that report before he met with his unwanted visitors.

Kelly handed William to Greta. "I'll get dressed and see what he wants."

"Not without me, you won't," Nick insisted. He turned to the nanny. "Call Zeke for me. I want him armed and outside my office. I also want a surveillance camera on Denny Russell until I can get in there. If Russell makes one wrong move, I want Zeke to call 911 and get the sheriff out here to arrest the man."

Kelly stared at him. "You really think Denny's dangerous?"

"We can't take the chance that he isn't."

BY THE TIME Kelly hurriedly dressed and headed out of her bedroom, she was a bundle of raw nerves. With this impromptu early-morning visit and Nick's cautious reaction, Kelly figured trouble could be just around the corner.

Nick was waiting for her just outside her suite door. He'd changed his clothes, as well, putting on jeans and a black shirt. He hadn't shaved, and that dark stubble made him look even more lethal than he usually did.

"I'd rather you not meet with Russell," Nick commented.

Kelly merely lifted her eyebrow. This meeting wasn't negotiable. She started down the hall, and Nick followed her.

As they approached Nick's office, she saw Zeke. The elderly ranch hand was in the open doorway, and he was indeed armed. He stepped to the side so that they could enter.

Nick went in first, naturally.

Though she'd held her ground about seeing Denny, Kelly had no plans to try to talk Nick out of his strong-arm mentality. Even though Denny was her friend and her late husband's former partner, Kelly wasn't in a trusting mood.

"Lattimer," Denny practically snarled. He put his hands on his hips. Definitely a defensive stance. "I came to see Kelly for a *private* conversation."

Nick didn't say a word, but his posture and expression said it all. He wasn't leaving.

"Why did you come, Denny?" Kelly asked.

Denny started toward her, but Nick blocked the man from getting too close. Kelly had to step to the side just so she could see Denny's face. Except his gaze was pinned on Nick.

They were a study in opposites. Denny with his sandy-blond military-cut hair. He was at least four inches shorter than Nick and bulkier. And while it was obvious that Denny was upset, his intensity level was nowhere near Nick's. Of course, not many people could ever match that level.

"I came because I'm worried about you," Denny explained. There was indeed some worry and concern in his dark-brown eyes. Plus, he looked rumpled and tired as if he hadn't slept. "And because I wanted to know how you were handling… things."

"You mean the lab results," Kelly provided. And she had to ask herself, how was she handling it? Probably not very well. She was a basket case and was getting emotionally involved with the man who would no doubt soon challenge her for custody of not only Joseph but William.

"I also mean the shooting," Denny continued. "The sheriff called and asked if I had an alibi."

"Do you?" Nick immediately asked.

"No." Denny's jaw and teeth clinched so tightly that she was surprised he could speak. "But that doesn't mean I'd fire shots at Kelly."

Kelly believed him, maybe because she wanted to.

But Denny had omitted any assurance that he wouldn't fire shots at Nick. She tried to imagine him doing something like that, but she just couldn't see him trying to kill anyone, especially if his motive was simply jealousy.

"I told Nick about the lab results," Kelly admitted to Denny. "I decided it wasn't a good idea for there to be secrets and lies between us. Not with so much at stake."

Oh, Denny did not like that. The displeasure coursed through his entire body, and his shoulders squared. "You trust Lattimer now?"

"Yes." And she didn't even have to think about it. She trusted him with her son. With her life. With her…she refused to finish that thought. She was already in enough trouble without adding romantic emotions to the mix. "Look, I'm safe here—"

"Safe! Safe?" Denny repeated. "How can you say that? You're not safe—someone shot at you."

"True, but Joseph and I are safer here than we would be anywhere else."

"That's not saying much. Kelly, I can take care of you and Joseph." His voice softened considerably, and he held out his hand to her. "Please give me the chance to do that."

The sigh that left her mouth was loud and long.

"Kelly and Joseph don't need you to protect

them," Nick snarled. "If you're truly her friend, then my suggestion is stay away from her until I can resolve the situation."

Denny slid his gaze in Nick's direction. "You mean with your brother?"

Nick didn't answer. Instead, he checked his watch. "I have other guests waiting for me. Zeke will show you out."

But Denny didn't leave. He reached out and took Kelly's arm. "Come with me. Please."

Kelly eased out of Denny's grip. "I can't."

Zeke stepped into the room, and it was his turn to grab Denny's arm. "The boss man said it's time to go, and that means you're going."

Denny ignored the man and kept his attention on her. "Don't you see? Nick Lattimer is dangerous, Kelly. He'll get you killed."

Then, with far more force than required, Denny flung off Zeke's grip and stormed out. Zeke followed to make sure he didn't backtrack.

Silence soon followed the conversational storm they'd just endured. Kelly wasn't sure what to say, but she started with the obvious. "I'm not sure it's necessary to treat Denny like a criminal."

"It is," Nick assured her. He took a folded piece of paper from the back pocket of his jeans. "This is the summary of a background check that I had Cooper run on Russell. I got it out of his office while you were dressing. Just how much do you know about his last days as a cop?"

She waited a moment so she could give that some thought. Kelly wasn't comfortable with where her thoughts led her. "I don't know much. He left SAPD a couple of weeks after Louis was killed."

"He didn't leave. He was forced to resign after an internal affairs investigation was launched into his conduct. The police thought Russell might have had something to do with your husband's death, but the evidence was inconclusive. Well, inconclusive about his being involved in the death. But they were able to prove that Russell interfered with the investigation by intimidating an informant into not testifying. In fact, the informant went into hiding and never resurfaced. That was enough for the police to demand Russell's resignation, but there wasn't enough hard evidence to officially charge him with a crime."

Her breath vanished. Sweet heaven, was it true? "Why didn't someone tell me?"

Nick shook his head. "I don't know. But until I find out more, I want you stay away from Russell. I don't want him in this house, and I don't want him around you."

She managed to nod. But she didn't want to stay away from Denny. Kelly wanted to run after him. She wanted to force him to tell her what'd happened. God. Had he really had some part in Louis's death?

She felt the tears threaten and knew that Nick didn't need her to cry on his shoulder again. She blinked hard, willing herself to keep her composure.

"I need some coffee," she said. Or maybe a shot of whiskey. Something to steady her nerves. "You go ahead and have your meeting with Paula and Todd."

He cupped her chin, lifted it and studied her eyes. "You'll be okay?"

"Of course," she lied.

But Kelly got out of there as quickly as she could and practically ran to her suite. She shut the door, buried her face in her hands and sank to the floor.

The memories of Louis's death came back to her like bullets. Brutal clips of information. The lieutenant coming to her door at two in the morning. One look at his face, and Kelly had known that Louis was dead. A drug bust gone bad, he'd said. Kelly hadn't asked for details. She feared each slam of bad news would put the fragile life that she was carrying inside her at risk.

The lieutenant had helped with funeral arrangements. Heck, he'd brought over a deli tray and phoned numerous times to ask how she was doing.

But he hadn't mentioned one thing about Denny being involved in Louis's death.

Looking back, the one person who'd been absent in those hours following Louis's death was Denny. In fact, it'd been days, maybe even weeks before he'd called her or come by to visit. Kelly hadn't thought much of it then.

Had Denny's friendship with her been spurred by guilt? She refused to believe he'd intentionally harmed Louis. But then…her mind went where she didn't want it to go. Denny had always been attracted to her. She'd known that on some deep level and had dismissed it because she was a married woman. What if Denny hadn't?

God.

What if he'd "removed" Louis from the picture with the hopes that he could get together with her? And now what if Denny was trying to do the same to Nick?

The sound of voices interrupted her thoughts. She stood and spotted the video baby monitor next to her bed. But the video feed wasn't coming from the nursery. The screen showed Nick's office. She walked closer and saw Nick in his meeting with Paula and Todd, the agents from the Justice Department. Nick had asked Greta to put a surveillance camera on Denny while he was in Nick's office, and someone had obviously forgotten to turn it off.

Kelly reached to turn off the monitor, but then she heard something that stopped her cold.

"This is our chance to finally get Eric," Todd said. "We have proof that he's been trying to assassinate a rival business associate—Marcus Durham."

"I know Marcus," Nick said. "We're old acquaintances. But I had no idea that Eric wants him dead." He shrugged. "Still, it doesn't surprise me. Marcus and Eric have clashed often on business deals. I'm sure Eric would do just about anything to prevent future opposition."

"And that's why we're here," Todd continued. "Like you, Marcus Durham is assisting the Justice Department with collecting information. We need him alive."

She watched as Nick shook his head. "I understand, but you still haven't said what you want me to do."

Todd opened his mouth, but Paula interrupted before he could answer.

"FYI, I didn't agree with this plan when our boss came up with it, and I don't agree with it now. It's too dangerous. Todd and I don't think you should go through with it." Paula no longer sounded like an agent. Her tone had a frantic, unprofessional edge to it.

Kelly knew she should turn off the monitor. This was a private conversation. But she couldn't make herself do it. After all, this concerned her, too.

"What's the plan?" Nick pressed.

"Our boss intends to plant information that Durham is about to seal a very lucrative deal that would seriously hurt Eric financially. The deal involves Durham's buy out of three companies that Eric needs for the manufacture and distribution of his heavy construction equipment. Durham will let Eric know that once he's the owner, he won't be doing business with him. Without those companies, Eric's construction equipment business will fail, and he'll lose over fifty percent of his income. That'll be the impetus to make Eric want to kill Durham even more."

"Maybe," Nick agreed. "But Eric will still need the opportunity to get to Marcus."

"And our boss wants you to create that opportunity," Todd explained. He wasn't frantic like his partner, but there was concern in his voice. "The Justice Department wants you to host a party for Marcus Durham so he can announce his engagement. We want Eric to believe he can use the occasion to come after Durham—especially since Eric hasn't been able to get around the elaborate security at Durham's estate."

Nick didn't say anything for several long moments. "You really think Eric would take the bait?"

"He wants Durham bad," Todd explained. "And the theory is that Eric won't be able to resist if you invite him to the party as well. Of course, you'll have to tell Eric to come alone so that he won't send one of his hired guns to do his dirty work."

She saw Nick's shoulders stiffen, and he shoved his thumb against his chest. "You want *me* to invite Eric here?"

"Yes," Paula snapped. She dropped down into the chair nearest Nick. "I told you I didn't like the plan.

Our boss thinks you can convince your brother that you want to bury the hatchet. I don't think you can."

"It doesn't matter what we think. This directive came down from above. The director thinks Eric will be more than willing to come once he learns that Durham will be here," Todd interjected, giving Paula a cool look. "Eric wants to kill Durham himself. He's said so to his inner circle of friends. This would be a perfect opportunity. And it would also be the perfect opportunity for us to catch Eric red-handed for attempted murder."

"Durham has agreed to this?" Nick asked.

"Reluctantly," Paula provided. She folded her arms over her chest. "He knows how important it is, but he's being cautious because he knows this could all backfire."

"What about Kelly and the babies? I wouldn't want them anywhere near Eric if we could somehow pull this off."

Again, it was Todd who answered. "We could move them to a safe house."

Oh, God. Nick was actually considering the plan.

And Kelly knew why he was considering it. It could be the chance to put Eric away so that Joseph and William would be safe. But the risk. Mercy, the risks to Nick would be astronomical.

"I'll do it," she heard Nick say.

Paula jumped to her feet. "Nick—"

"I have to try," he interrupted. "I have to do whatever I can to keep Kelly and the boys safe." Nick paused and aimed his attention at Todd. "But this stays in this room. I don't want Kelly to know about anything we've discussed. She has enough on her mind without adding this."

Kelly's stomach tightened, and she automatically moved closer to the monitor. Had she heard Nick correctly?

"I think that's wise," Todd concluded. "No reason to tell her. It would only make her worry."

Paula huffed. "Then you better say your goodbyes now, Nick. Because once this party gets started, there's no assurance, *none,* that we can keep you alive."

Chapter Thirteen

Kelly stood there in her suite. Stunned. She couldn't believe what she'd just heard.

Nick was going to use himself and that other man as bait.

And he was going to lie to her about the danger.

That stung. Nick didn't believe she was strong enough to handle the truth. Or maybe he just thought he was doing her a favor by keeping her in the dark. His life would be on the line, and if she hadn't overheard that conversation, she never would have understood why he'd shipped her and the babies off to a safe house.

She groaned. Obviously, Nick and she weren't making much headway in a relationship if he didn't trust her with the truth.

Kelly threw open the door to her room. She wanted to confront Nick. Actually, she wanted to yell at him. And the two Justice Department agents.

But then Kelly saw Greta coming down the hall with both boys in a double stroller.

"I just had it delivered," Greta said motioning toward the stroller.

"It's really nice," Kelly said. And she hoped she sounded sincere, because it was nice. Both the stroller and the fact that Greta had ordered it.

"I was about to take them to the solarium," Greta explained. "I thought they might like a little sunshine."

"Would you mind if I did it?" Not only would it mean being with Joseph and William, Kelly could use the time to try to figure out what she was going to do about Nick. She definitely needed a cooling-off period.

Smiling, Greta passed the stroller to her. Since Kelly couldn't quite manage a smile, she hurried away. Thankfully, the babies wouldn't notice her sour mood.

She followed the hall to the east side of the house and the massive solarium. The room was filled with greenery and flowering plants in richly colored terracotta pots. It was a stark contrast to the winter landscape outside.

There was a circular path of sorts made of beautiful Mexican tiles, and Kelly pushed the stroller along it so the babies could see the flowers. Joseph pointed to a pot of scarlet roses and babbled something. He turned to her and smiled.

With a smile forming on her own lips, she heard

the sound of footsteps. She reeled around and saw Zeke, the ranch hand.

"You doing okay in here?" he asked.

Greta had no doubt sent him to check on her.

"I'm okay." It was almost true. Almost. "Is it safe to go to the stables?"

"Afraid not. Did you want to go riding?"

"No." She couldn't say that quickly enough. "Actually, I'm scared of horses. I just thought if I managed to see one up close that the fear might go away."

She was babbling. Sheez. Since Nick had jokingly made that comment about not getting involved with a woman with a fear of horses or cows, she'd been obsessed with the notion of becoming more comfortable around livestock.

The corner of Zeke's mouth hitched. "Maybe I can teach you to ride when things settle down around here." He tipped his head to Joseph. "That's Nick's boy, isn't it? Don't bother answering. I can see it. Of course, the problem is Nick's snake of a brother can see it, too."

Yes. Eric no doubt could. And that made her realize something. Nick was desperate to keep the babies safe. She certainly was. That desperation had likely caused him to agree to Todd's plan to have this dangerous party. Nick was doing it again. He was risking his own life for theirs.

Kelly suddenly felt lower than dirt.

Here she'd had thoughts about yelling at him for another lie when she knew in her heart that the lie was for the best of reasons. Nick hadn't buried his head in the sand over his brother. He was taking action.

"Enjoy your stroll, Ms. Manning," Zeke said, giving both boys' tummies a goose. Joseph and William giggled.

As she watched Zeke stroll away, Kelly had to admit that her mood had improved significantly. Strange. There was still so much hanging over them that she wasn't sure a good mood was the safest attitude to take.

She stopped by some potted trees and realized the small fruit growing on them were lemons. She automatically smiled. There was something amusing about a Texas cowboy who grew lemons.

She glanced down at the babies to make sure they were okay, and time seemed to freeze. Kelly heard a deafening crash.

She turned, saw the glass flying right toward her, and automatically dove forward to shelter William and Joseph. She landed hard against the stroller, not a second too soon.

The dangerous shards of glass spewed over the solarium and pelted her.

Even then her mind didn't register what'd

happened. Not until there was a second blast, and a second storm of flying glass.

That's when she knew someone was shooting at them.

NICK WAS ON HOLD WAITING for an update about Cooper when he heard the sound.

A sound that shot terror straight through him.

He dropped the phone on his desk, grabbed his gun and started to run. He'd barely made it out of his office when he heard the second crash.

Hell.

He prayed that the sound of shattering glass didn't mean that someone was trying to break in.

He raced down the hall, looking in each room. There was no sign of Kelly, the babies or Greta. And that did nothing to calm his fears.

"They're in the solarium," he heard Zeke yell. The man was armed with a rifle.

Nick rushed past Zeke and made a beeline for the solarium. However, he didn't immediately see Kelly because there was another thick blast, followed by yet more spewing glass.

Sharp pieces of glass that could do some serious harm.

"Kelly?" Nick called out.

"Over here." Her voice sounded strained and muffled. God, he hoped that didn't mean she was hurt.

Nick followed the sound of her voice and realized she was in the far corner of the room. There was at least fifty feet of glass and plants between them. That didn't stop him. Nothing would. One way or the other, he was getting to Kelly and their sons.

"Stay down," Nick yelled. He glanced at Zeke. "Call the sheriff and try to see who the hell is trying to kill us."

Zeke nodded and hurried off. Nick turned his full attention to getting across the room. He took a deep breath, said a prayer and, while crouching as low as he could, he began to make his way toward Kelly.

There was another shot.

And another.

Nick figured the bullets had been fired from a long-range rifle. The shooter was probably either perched on a barn or else in a tree in the heavily wooded area just beyond the fence. Either way, the person was in a position to keep firing.

Bullets crashed through what was left of the east wall of the solarium. But the glass wasn't all the bullets hit. The terracotta pots were smashed, as well, and dirt, plants and jagged clay pieces exploded in the air. Nick had to duck his head to protect his eyes.

Both boys were crying, shrieking with terror.

"Are you hurt?" he asked Kelly.

She didn't answer, and with each passing second, Nick's heart pounded harder.

"I think we're okay," she finally said.

Think. Which meant she wasn't certain. And that sent his fears and heart racing out of control.

The shots continued, a barrage of deadly gunfire. Nick ducked the flying pottery pieces and continued his race to get to Kelly. When he finally spotted her amid the debris and chaos, she was hovered in the corner, on the side of two lemon trees, and she was using her body to shield the babies.

"I'm here," Nick let her know.

He maneuvered himself between her and the east side of the house where the shots were coming from. And he turned so he could try to do something about that damn shooter.

Nick frantically searched the barn tops but didn't see anyone, especially not a gunman armed with a scope rifle. He kept looking. Until he finally spotted what he thought might be sunlight dancing off metal. A glimmer, that's all it was. And it was indeed coming from one of the massive oaks just on the other side of the pasture fence.

Though it was useless, Nick moved slightly away from Kelly, took aim and fired. He wished like hell that he'd taken the rifle from Zeke. It would have been a lot more effective than his handgun.

"I need to get you out of here," Nick told her. Though there was no way he could safely do that. Still, he had to try. Each shot had the potential to kill them.

Nick positioned himself in the line of fire, and he reached behind him to grab the stroller handle. "Keep as low as possible," he instructed Kelly.

"The sheriff's on the way," Zeke shouted.

Thank God. But the sheriff's arrival was still minutes away. A lot could happen during that time.

"Zeke, the shooter's on the other side of the pasture fence. Fire a few shots in that direction so I can get Kelly and the babies out of here."

Zeke used the door frame for cover, aimed the rifle through the shattered glass and fired. The loud, thundering blast only caused the boys to cry even harder.

Nick hurried Kelly and the babies toward safety while Zeke continued to fire. Nick cursed when a ceramic pot shattered right in front of them. He glanced back at Kelly to make sure no one was hurt. He didn't see any blood, but he did see the look of terror on her face. She was ashen pale, trembling, but there was also some fierce determination in her expression.

And just like that, the gunman's shots stopped.

"YOU'RE NOT GOING out there," Sheriff Cross insisted, catching Nick's arm to stop him from leaving.

That didn't please Nick one bit. He wanted nothing more than to grab a Glock and a hunting rifle and go after the SOB who'd just attacked Kelly and their sons.

"That whole area is now a crime scene," the sheriff

continued, releasing the grip he had on him. "I want a chance to look for footprints and other evidence. And I can't do that if you're out there with guns blazing."

Nick couldn't deny that he'd do just that. If he saw the shooter, he would definitely try to take him out.

Kelly stepped in front of him. "Let's make sure Greta got the boys settled down."

Her voice was still shaky. Because she was so close, he could feel her every muscle trembling. With reason. They'd all come damn close to dying.

This was Eric's doing. Well, probably. But Nick couldn't discount Denny Russell.

"You said your two visitors left just about a half hour ago?" Sheriff Cross asked before Nick and Kelly could leave to check on the boys.

Nick nodded. "Paula Barker and Todd Burgess."

"After I've gone over the crime scene, I'll want to talk to them."

So did Nick. And he wanted to talk to Cooper, as well. "Their phone numbers are in the Rolodex in my office. One of the housekeepers can get them for you."

Nick didn't explain that Paula and Todd were federal agents. He'd let them tell Sheriff Cross that particular detail. That way, the Justice Department could decide how much they wanted the local authorities to know.

"Have Greta stay put in the panic room," the

sheriff continued. "You two might want to stand guard outside just in case."

"You think that gunman is coming back?" Kelly touched her fingers to her mouth.

"There's always a chance of something like that. Lock yourself in and stay put. I'll call you on your cell phone and let you know when it's okay to come out."

Cross didn't have to say it twice. The panic room was safe, but the rest of the house obviously wasn't. Someone could get in. Someone that Eric had hired to get Joseph. Nick had to make sure that didn't happen.

Kelly and Nick hurried to the nursery, and he got her a weapon from the safe. Nick threw open the closet door that led to the panic room. Rather than rush in and frighten the babies and Greta even more than they already had been, he used the tiny monitor next to the keypad for the panic room entrance. The image quickly popped up on the screen. Not an image of chaos or pandemonium. Both boys were asleep on quilts on the floor, and Greta was in the rocking chair next to them.

He pressed the intercom button. "Kelly and I are at the top of the stairs," he whispered to Greta. "We're keeping the door locked. And we're standing guard until the sheriff gives us the okay. If you need anything, just ask."

Greta nodded, and in just that simple gesture, Nick

could see the tension and the fear. It was a good thing that the babies seemed calm and happy.

Kelly touched the screen, running her fingers over the image of first Joseph and then William. "It's a miracle they weren't hurt."

Yeah. And Nick hated to rely on miracles when it came to their safety.

"I was so scared when the bullets were flying," Kelly said, her voice choppy now. She had a gun in her right hand, but she fisted her left one and pushed it hard against her forehead. "I thought the boys were going to die. I thought *you* were going to die."

The only light was coming from the monitor, but Nick had no trouble seeing the tears in her eyes. Not surprising. She'd just survived a trip to hell and back.

"We have to stop Eric," she added.

"We will. *I* will," Nick corrected, putting his arm around her.

She choked back a sob and threw herself against him. Nick had braced himself for that to happen. The adrenaline was no doubt still racing through her, and she probably felt ready to explode. He certainly did. He was primed and ready for a fight, and there was no one or nowhere he could aim that dangerous energy.

"No one was hurt," Nick reminded her. "The babies are safe."

"But for how long?" It wasn't the question of a

defeated woman. She was furious. "I want to kill Eric for this. I want to make him pay for what he tried to do to William and Joseph."

Her breath broke. A hoarse moan came from deep within her throat. She jammed her fist against his chest.

Nick kissed her before she lost it and before her tears could spill down her cheeks. It definitely wasn't the time for a kiss, but he didn't know what else to do. He figured Kelly would push him away or yell at him, anything to redirect that energy.

But she didn't. Kelly returned the kiss with a vengeance.

It was as if she took all her fear, anger and frustration and poured it into that kiss. This wasn't romantic. Heck, it was barely even sexual. But she apparently needed that kiss because when Nick tried to break away so he could ask if she was all right, Kelly held on for dear life.

Nick held on, as well. Because he needed her, needed this contact as much as she obviously did.

The kiss became deep and hot. Nick responded in the most basic male way. He stopped thinking if this was the right or wrong thing to do, and just went with what was happening.

Kelly plastered herself against him, and she coiled her arms around him. Nick did some arm wrapping himself, and even though they couldn't get much closer, he tried. Because getting closer suddenly seemed more important to him than his next breath.

She said his name. It was a thick, breathy whisper. And she slid her hand between them so she could touch his erection. It was like striking a match. The flames soared. And Nick knew despite the consequences, they were already at the point of no return.

He turned and pushed her back against the wall. He wasn't gentle. Neither was she. It wasn't the time for that. The need was too demanding. The emotions too high. They both just wanted release, and they wanted it now.

Nick scooped her up, and she automatically adjusted herself so that her legs were on each side of his hips. She wore a slim green dress, which Nick was thankful for.

Her legs were bare, and he could feel the soft skin of her inner thighs. He didn't take the time to savor it. He didn't take the time to savor anything. They fought to rid her of her panties and lower his zipper.

Now, now, now—that was the only word in his head, and it pounded in cadence with their heartbeats.

He entered her the moment she freed him from his boxer briefs. He slid in hot and deep. They paused for only a moment. One too-short moment so that he could force himself to be gentle.

But Kelly didn't want gentle.

She moved against him. Hard. Fast. Nick didn't

even try to reset the pace or resist this avalanche of
need. He just went with it. He thrust himself into her,
again and again, until everything pinpointed into a
demand for release. That was it. Nothing else
mattered, only release.

"Now," he said.

But Kelly was already going there. She moved her
hips against him one last time. It was a hard, frantic
motion that racked her entire body.

He felt her climax, and he followed suit. One last
thrust into that warm, wet heat, and he knew he
couldn't make this last. He buried his face against her
neck and let himself go.

Chapter Fourteen

Kelly's breath was coming out in rough gusts, and her heart rate had to be off the scale. Still, she forced herself to come back to earth.

And the impact of what she'd just done hit her full force.

"Oh, hell," Nick mumbled.

He, too, had obviously realized that having sex against the closet wall wasn't the smartest thing they could have done. Yet neither of them had been able to do anything to stop it.

Kelly wiggled out of his grip and put her feet back on the floor. She quickly located her panties, put them on and fixed her dress so that it wasn't around her waist. Nick adjusted his clothes, too, and then looked behind him to check the monitor. Nothing had changed. The babies were still asleep. They were safe.

No thanks to him.

They'd been having sex while they should have been standing guard.

"I can't believe we just did that," Kelly mumbled.

He made a sound to indicate he agreed. "It was an adrenaline reaction." It was as good an excuse as any, especially since he wasn't eager to discuss it.

Kelly wanted to know what it all meant. If anything. But this wasn't the time or the place for a conversation about how this would change their relationship.

He retrieved his gun and pressed in some keys on the monitor. He scanned through his office—it was empty. Next he viewed the kitchen, where the cook was looking out the window. And finally he switched to the exterior cameras. She saw the sheriff and his deputies. They were searching the ground for something. Spent shell casings maybe. The sheriff was also talking on his cell phone.

Nick scanned more of the grounds before he switched back to the nursery. There still wasn't much activity going on there, and that meant there wasn't much to focus on. The silence and the tension soon became thick.

"I'm sorry," Nick said.

"For what?"

He stared at her a moment. "For having sex with you." His eyes widened. "Unprotected sex."

Kelly was sure her eyes widened, as well, but she

fought through the feeling of panic and forced herself to do the math. "It's the wrong time of the month," she let him know. "And as for STDs, I'm clear there, too. It'll be okay."

But Nick's expression said otherwise.

Mercy, what had they done?

They'd just started to feel comfortable with each other. They'd just started to develop trust. Now this was going to create more issues between them.

"We can pretend it didn't happen," she suggested.

"Is that what you want?" he retorted.

Kelly didn't know what she wanted when it came to Nick, and she didn't have a chance to talk about that with him.

Nick's phone rang, the sound shooting through the otherwise silent room. He snatched it from his pocket.

"It's the sheriff," he said glancing down at the caller ID on the screen. "Did you find the gunman?" Nick demanded when he answered the call.

The answer was obviously no because Nick's scowl deepened. He clicked off the phone. "The sheriff's coming back to the house."

That was her cue to double-check to make sure her clothes were straight and that she didn't look as if she'd just had sex with Nick. The first was doable, but she doubted the second was. She only hoped the sheriff didn't notice.

Nick opened the door that led into the nursery, and

Kelly had just enough time to check her hair and face in the mirror before Sheriff Cross came in.

"Well?" Nick asked.

"There's no sign of the gunman. But you were right. He or she was in a tree just on the other side of the fence. This doesn't look like the work of an amateur. The area was clean. Too clean. Someone didn't want to leave behind any incriminating evidence."

That caused her stomach to knot. A professional gunman had just tried to kill her and the babies. But then, she hadn't expected anything less from Eric. He wouldn't have hired anyone but a pro to do this job.

"I got the phone numbers for Paula Barker and Todd Burgess and called them while I was outside," the sheriff explained. "They said they left your place alone and in separate vehicles. Miss Barker was in a white two-door. Mr. Burgess in a light-gray sedan. Any reason to suspect that one of them might have doubled back and taken shots at the house?"

That knot in Kelly's stomach got worse.

"I don't think so," Nick answered. What he didn't mention was that Paula and Todd were federal agents. That would have to come out sooner or later. Once Sheriff Cross knew who the duo was, he probably wouldn't suspect them of a crime.

"My deputies are questioning the ranch hands," Sheriff Cross continued. "One of them claims to have seen a light-colored car on that dirt road on the back of your property. It was hidden behind some trees, so the ranch hand didn't get a good look at it."

"Why didn't he report this to me before the shooting?" Nick snarled.

"He said he thought it was no big deal, that since that acreage is for sale, it might've been a possible buyer looking at the land." The sheriff paused. "Since Ms. Barker and Mr. Burgess were driving light-colored cars, I wondered if it could be one of them."

"I don't know any reason why they'd be back there." Nick shook his head and shoved his hand through his hair. "I'm not sure who to trust. Cooper, my security manager, is nowhere to be found, and this is the second attempt on our lives in the past two days."

The sheriff bobbed his head. "Yeah, it's obvious that someone wants to hurt you, and even if your brother's behind these attacks, it's my guess that he's not the shooter."

"No," Nick mumbled.

Kelly agreed. She didn't know Eric, but he probably wouldn't want to dirty his own hands unless it was absolutely necessary.

"I'll make this investigation a top priority," the sheriff said. "My advice—disappear for a while. Or if you stay here, hire some extra security."

The sheriff headed out. Kelly and Nick stood there, silently, but Nick didn't need to say anything for her to know what he was thinking.

"The shootings will continue until we stop Eric," Nick said under his breath.

"Yes."

Now the question was—how did they stop him? And how did they figure out if he had some outside help? Like Rosalinda McMillan, Eric's former secretary perhaps? Or Cooper, Nick's own security manager?

Or heaven forbid, her friend Denny.

"What about Paula and Todd?" she asked. "Is there a reason why they would have taken those shots?"

He opened his mouth, and it seemed as if he were about to say no, but he stopped. "I guess it's possible that Eric could have gotten to one of them."

That realization went through her entire body, and Kelly felt her legs go weak. "God. You're right. But Eric could have gotten to anyone, even Cooper or Denny."

"You know what I have to do," Nick said. He turned, looked at her.

She nodded. "I know."

"I'll get some extra guards out here as the sheriff suggested. But once I'm sure the place is secure, I'll set up the party and call Eric. If I can get him to take the bait, all of this could all be over by tomorrow night."

But Kelly knew that was being overly optimistic. By tomorrow night Nick could be facing the most dangerous situation of his life, and there was nothing she could do to protect him.

THE PLANS for the party were well underway. The cook had already arranged for a caterer. Extra staff and security guards were being brought in. Nick had even worked out the situation with Kelly. Greta, she and the babies would be in the bulletproof panic room, with not one but two security guards stationed outside. Kelly would be armed, and she would have emergency communication equipment. The only thing left to do was call Eric and try to talk him into coming.

But first Nick had to take a deep breath.

He wasn't immune to the dangerous situation this party could create, and even though Nick was taking every precaution possible, nothing was a hundred percent. Kelly and the babies could still get hurt. That's why he'd considered asking the Justice Department to provide a safe house for them. But after a lengthy conversation with Kelly, Nick had opted for the panic room instead because they agreed that in the long run it would be safer. At least they would be closer to him in case he was needed.

Nick prayed it wasn't a huge mistake.

He also hoped that having sex with Kelly hadn't been an equally bad mistake. He'd been wrong to take her that way. She'd been scared and vulnerable, and he'd ignored that and had sex with her anyway. He wasn't proud of what he'd done, even though he sure as hell didn't know how he could have stopped it.

Or how he could make himself not want her again.

Once he had the situation with Eric under control, he really needed to sit down with Kelly so they could work out some things.

Nick reached for the phone again, just as there was a soft knock at his door. "It's me," Kelly said peeking around the corner of the door.

"Come in," he offered.

Actually, she was a welcome sight and a reprieve from the phone call he had to make. She'd changed her clothes since the incident in the closet and now wore jeans and a lemon-yellow pullover sweater. The color made her whole face glow. Or maybe the sex had had something to do with that.

Was that wishful thinking on his part?

Nick didn't know how to feel about what they'd done, but he figured it would come back to bite him in the butt. Lapses in judgment usually did. It wasn't that he regretted sex with her per se, but he did regret the distraction.

And sex with Kelly had been the ultimate distraction.

"How are the babies?" he asked.

"Fine. Greta and I just finished giving them lunch. They ate well. William loves peas."

She smiled. Nick smiled, too, because it was obvious that she was enjoying the whole process of getting to know her son. He would enjoy it, too, once he had some other things in order—namely their safety.

"Joseph prefers fruit," she volunteered. "Pears especially, but if it's yellow and gooey, then he won't put up a fuss about eating it."

"Pears," Nick repeated. He'd make sure they were on the baby menu tonight. In fact, he wanted to do a lot of things to make tonight special.

The calm before the storm of the party.

"Are you okay?" he asked.

"Yes. You?"

"I'm okay." Both knew they'd just told huge white lies. "I was about to call Eric to see if he'd accept the invitation to the party."

She nodded and moistened her lips. Her shoulders went back as if she were bracing herself. Nick mentally prepared himself, as well.

He pressed in the numbers to Eric's private line. It wasn't the first time Nick had called it. There'd been a flurry of calls after William's birth. But those calls had been to assure his brother that there was no risk to his precious inheritance. Other times, the calls had been threats. Mainly from Nick to Eric.

The threats obviously hadn't worked.

He hoped this party invitation had better results.

"Nick," Eric greeted. He'd obviously checked his caller ID. "Did you call to apologize for ordering me off your beloved ranch?"

"Not a chance." Nick wasn't sure if this was the correct way to play this, but he went with his gut feel. Eric would get suspicious if he groveled or apologized.

Eric stayed quiet for several moments. "What do you want, then?" he finally asked. "Because as you well know, we have nothing to say to each other."

"Agreed. But this isn't about me. I'm calling to invite you to a party to celebrate Marcus Durham's engagement. Trust me, it wasn't my idea. Marcus wants you there."

"Why?" And Eric didn't waste any time asking it, either.

"Well, it could be because you two were once old friends, but knowing Marcus, there's probably another reason. He's engaged to one of your former lovers, and I figure Marcus wants to use the occasion to rub it in your face that he got the woman that you couldn't keep."

"He got my leftovers," Eric snarled. "If I'd wanted to keep Cecelia, I would have."

So, his brother hadn't needed a clarification of which lover, but then, Marcus had been keeping company with Eric's old flames for several years now.

"Let me get this straight," Eric continued. "This is an impromptu party, and Marcus wants me there. You know I'm suspicious, right?"

"That goes without saying," Nick confirmed. "I'm

suspicious, too, and I've warned Marcus that he'd better not use this occasion to start anything with you. I don't want violence in my home."

"Violence, huh? Now that's an interesting possibility. I've heard rumors that Marcus might not have my best interests at heart. I've been wanting to discuss that with him."

"This party won't be the place to do that," Nick lied. Was his brother actually going to agree to come? If so, it was time to announce the major ground rule. "If you come, you come alone, without your so-called bodyguards."

"What about Marcus? Will he be without his *bodyguards,* as well?"

"Of course."

"Of course," Eric repeated. "Well, this invitation sounds tempting and all, but I don't want to go where I'm not welcome by the host."

"If you're waiting for me to welcome you with open arms, it's not going to happen. It's Marcus that wants you here, but since he's a friend, I told him that I thought we were both man enough to tolerate each other for an hour or two."

Nick left it at that. He didn't dare push more to get his brother to come, or Eric would almost certainly become more suspicious.

"I'll give it some thought," Eric finally said. "And I'll get back to you."

Nick hung up the phone, and he met Kelly's gaze. "He'll let me know."

Her shoulders dropped. "What if he says no?"

"Then we come up with a different plan. We'll stop him, Kelly." And Nick had to believe that was true. Because there was no other alternative.

Kelly stuffed her hands into the back pockets of her snug jeans. The little maneuver tightened her sweater over her breasts, which reminded him that he'd yet to see her breasts. That speed-sex session hadn't left any time for foreplay.

He frowned and mumbled some profanity under his breath. Now wasn't the time to think about such things.

"I can't get it off my mind, either," Kelly whispered.

His gaze came to hers again, and he decided it was a good time to stay quiet until she clarified that. This was a case where he could definitely insert his foot into his mouth.

"Closet sex," she added.

Ah, so they were thinking the same thing. Not good. It would have been nice for at least one of them not to be ruled by this six-hundred-pound gorilla of an attraction.

"I'm giving you an out," she said.

Nick blinked. "A what?"

"An out. I don't want you to feel that this has to change anything. For the good or the bad. We can consider it just a lapse. That's all."

It seemed a little more than a lapse, but Nick kept that to himself.

"I don't do that sort of thing," Kelly continued. "My life is usually pretty routine." She paused. "Well, it was until I found out about the baby switch."

He made a sound of agreement. "And that brought me into your life."

She waited a moment. "Are you trying to figure out if that's a good or bad thing?"

"Definitely good." But then, he groaned. "But not good for you. Because of me, your life is in danger."

"No. My life's in danger because of Eric." She walked closer, took her hands from her pockets. She reached out, but then obviously had second thoughts. "Touching you is probably not a good idea."

But that didn't stop Nick.

He pulled her into his arms. The embrace didn't feel sexual. It felt far more intimate than that, and despite his insistence that intimacy or sex was not an option, Nick still felt that kick.

That need for more.

But there was a knock at the door, and Kelly pulled away from him. The look in her eyes told him that she was dreading more bad news.

"Yes?" Nick called out.

"It's me—Cooper."

Nick didn't know which he felt most—surprise or anger. It was probably an even mix of both.

Cooper didn't wait for an invitation to enter. He opened the door and stepped inside. His clothes were rumpled, and he hadn't shaved.

Nick didn't let down his guard over Cooper's disheveled appearance. He took Kelly by the arm and pulled her behind him. He also drew his gun.

Cooper eyed the gun before his stunned eyes met Nick's. "You think that's necessary?"

"I don't know if I can trust you. Where the hell have you been?"

Cooper sighed heavily, and wearily scrubbed his hand over his bald head. "You probably aren't going to believe this, but someone kidnapped me. For the past twenty-four hours, I've been locked in the trunk of my car while it was parked on Crenshaw Bluff."

"Crenshaw Bluff," Nick repeated, hoping he sounded as skeptical as he felt. "What were you doing there?"

"I got a call from someone who claimed he was Eric's chauffeur. He said he had some info about his boss that I might want. So I drove all the way out there, got out of my car and the next thing I know, someone used a stun gun on me. When I came to, I was locked in the truck of my car, and the escape lever had been disabled so I couldn't get out. Thankfully, eventually some hikers heard me yelling and got me out."

Nick weighed each word carefully and stared at

the man that he'd once trusted with his life. "Why would someone do this to you?"

But Nick already knew the answer. Maybe Eric wanted Cooper out of the way so he could orchestrate that attack in the solarium. That scenario certainly smacked of Eric.

"You don't believe me," Cooper said. And then his attention landed on Kelly. "Are you responsible for this? Have you turned him against me?"

"No, she hasn't," Nick insisted. But he might as well have been talking to the wind because he could see the venom in Cooper's eyes.

"It might be a good idea for you to take some vacation time," Nick suggested. "It'll give you a chance to recover from your ordeal."

"I don't need to recover. And I don't need a damn vacation. I need you to believe me."

Nick shook his head. "I don't have time to sort through what happened. And I can't blindly trust you anymore because someone tried to kill us— again. What I need is for you to leave. Temporarily. And when I've worked out some things, we'll talk."

"I don't care what you say," Cooper grumbled. "She's to blame for this. Can't you see it, Nick? Ever since she came here, your life has been a living hell. My advice? Take your son and leave before it's too late."

"Which son?" Nick questioned. "The one I raised or the one I fathered? Because I love them both equally. And that's why you're leaving. Because I don't know if I can trust you to be around them." Nick paused a heartbeat. "Please don't make me escort you off the property."

It hurt Nick to say that. Cooper and he had been together for nearly seven years. But he wasn't about to put Cooper's feelings above Kelly and the babies' safety.

"I'll leave," Cooper assured him. "But I thought you'd like to know that I finally dug up some info on the baby swap."

"I'm listening," Nick assured him.

"Meredith knew she was dying, and she paid one of the doctors at the birthing center to switch your son with the next infant boy to be born. It just happened to be Kelly's son."

Nick wasn't surprised. He understood Meredith's reasons for doing what she did, but that swap had created a totally new set of problems.

Cooper didn't issue any veiled threats. Nor did he aim any more of that venom at Kelly. He simply shook his head, turned and walked out.

"I'm sorry," Kelly said.

"For what?"

"For coming between the two of you."

"You didn't. If Cooper's innocent, we'll work it

out like I said. But if he's guilty, then I don't want him anywhere around you or our…sons."

The corner of her mouth lifted into a very brief smile. "You know, I feel the same way about Joseph and William. I love them both equally."

Yes. He didn't doubt that. But he did wonder how they were going to work out raising the children, when it was obvious they both wanted to be full-time parents. Later, maybe Nick could devote some time to figuring out that particular issue.

But that couldn't happen now.

The phone rang again. First, Nick went to the door and locked it. He didn't want Cooper to rethink his semi-civil exit and return for round two. Then he returned to his desk and looked down at his caller ID.

It was Eric.

Kelly joined him, side by side, and she too glanced at the screen. "He must have decided whether or not he's going to come."

Nick wasn't counting on it. His brother loved to play games, and Eric might have sensed that this was the ultimate game.

Nick pressed the speakerphone function. "Well?" he greeted.

"Satan is probably wearing a parka right now because hell is freezing over as we speak," Eric commented.

"And why is that?" Nick asked.

"Because I accept your *heartfelt* invitation to attend Marcus's party."

The sarcasm dripped from Eric's voice. But the sarcasm wasn't all Nick heard. He also heard the eagerness. Eric must have fought hard not to jump at the invitation right away. Oh, yeah. He wanted Marcus dead and figured this was the opportunity to do it.

Kelly pulled in her breath, and Nick glanced at her to see how she was handling this. No sarcasm or eagerness for her. Just fear and concern. Nick totally understood that.

"What time is this shindig?" Eric asked.

"Tomorrow night. Eight o'clock. Don't expect to stay long, because your particular invitation is only for a quick toast and an equally quick exit."

Eric chuckled. "Trust me, I don't want to spend much time there, either. Marcus and I just need to get a few things straight." He paused. No more chuckling. "Oh, and Nick, if this is some kind of trick, you'll pay for it in the worst way possible."

"The same applies to you," Nick countered. He hoped he sounded calm and confident because he certainly didn't feel those things.

He stabbed the end call button.

Things were really in motion now. He was responsible for that. Nick only hoped that he could survive so he could keep Kelly, William and Joseph alive.

Nick rifled through his desk drawer and came up with the number he was looking for.

"Who are you calling?" Kelly asked as he pressed in the numbers.

"The unit director at the Justice Department. Gideon Tate." Nick had met the man only briefly, but Nick had had him thoroughly investigated. For what it was worth, Gideon seemed as trustworthy as possible.

He put this call on speakerphone, as well. That way, Kelly could hear what he intended to do.

"The party is on schedule," Nick informed Gideon. "My brother just accepted the invitation."

"Well done. I wasn't sure you could pull it off."

Nick glanced at Kelly who lifted her eyebrow. "Neither was I." He paused. "I'm obviously concerned about safety."

"Of course you are. I'll assign six agents to this. Their sole mission will be to keep Marcus Durham, you and the other members of your household safe. If possible, we want to arrest Eric once we've established intent to commit murder. We'd like that to happen before any weapons are fired. Just in case, though, both Marcus Durham and you will wear Kevlar bulletproof vests, and you'll both be armed."

"Good. I want three of those agents assigned to keep Kelly Manning and the two infant boys safe. But I do have another demand. I don't want Todd or

Paula anywhere near the ranch until this situation with Eric is resolved."

That caused Kelly to lift another eyebrow. Nick touched her arm to reassure her that he knew what he was doing.

"What happened to make you feel this way?" Gideon asked.

"The shooting at my ranch for one thing. I don't know if I can trust Paula and Todd any longer. I'm worried that Eric might have gotten to one or both of them."

"There's no evidence of that." And Gideon didn't hesitate, either.

"That's not enough. Evidence can be hidden, and I don't want to take any unnecessary risks. Right now Paula and Todd are definite risks as far as I'm concerned."

"All right," the director said hesitantly. "I'll assign a new team. One that I'll personally handpick. But you do know there are no guarantees. If Eric can get to Paula and Todd, he can get to anyone."

Yes. Nick was fully aware of that. And that's why he had to play his own deadly game. A double cross, of sorts. Because although he didn't trust Paula, Todd, Cooper or Denny, he didn't trust Gideon, either. Not after the continued attempts to kill them.

That meant, for better or worse, Kelly and he were on their own.

Chapter Fifteen

Kelly sipped her sparkling Italian white wine. Though it was her favorite, it didn't help her relax. Neither had the expensive-smelling bubble bath Nick had left in her suite. But then, it was going to take a lot more than a bath and a glass of wine to ease the tension that throbbed in her temples and back. It would likely be there until this blasted party had run its course.

Giving up on the bath, she set her glass aside, stepped from the massive whirlpool tub, dried off and put on her robe. Someone on Nick's staff had retrieved it from her house. She hugged the soft yellow terry cloth to her body, sighed and finally sank down into the chair by the vanity. There was a monitor there, and Kelly flipped through the various camera angles until she located Nick.

He was in the nursery "reading" to the boys.

Nick had one baby nestled in the crook of each of

his arms. Both Joseph and William were sound asleep, but Nick continued to sit there and read to them. He was obviously enjoying fatherhood. Which, of course, immediately brought to mind the next question: Would he continue to enjoy it?

And she was back to the one thing she didn't want to think about tonight. The party. Yet, it was the very thing she couldn't get off her mind. Eric could be arrested and put in jail. Maybe that would end the threats.

And maybe Eric would just continue his reign of terror from behind bars. Even a life sentence in a maximum security prison might not even slow him down.

Of course, the party could make things worse. If Eric caught onto the fact that it was a setup, he might storm out and escalate his threats. But then, things couldn't get much more escalated than having shots fired at them.

Movement on the screen grabbed her attention. Somehow, Nick managed to get to his feet. Without waking either child, he placed them in their respective cribs and covered them with blankets. Both boys got kisses on the foreheads.

Kelly couldn't help but smile.

And dream.

At the moment it was one heck of a pipe dream, but she let herself imagine what it would be like to witness a scene like that every night. Nick and she raising their sons. Without the threat of Eric. With nothing but time for them to work out where all of this was going.

But personal stuff seemed trivial compared to death threats and murder attempts, and Kelly longed for the day when she might have the opportunity to figure out if Nick and she might take this relationship farther than French kisses and closet sex.

There was a knock at the door, and Kelly automatically glanced at the monitor screen. Nick was no longer in the nursery, so she figured he might be the one at her bathroom door.

"Come in," she offered.

The door opened, and there he was. He wasn't smiling exactly, but he looked content. And rather rumpled. His hair was a little disheveled, and he had a hot-desperado, five-o'clock-shadow thing going on. Just looking at him caused the heat to roll through her.

Of course, thinking about him had the same effect.

"Is that pear on your shirt?" she asked, forcing herself not to think of the heat.

Nick glanced down at the smeared stain on his white shirt. "Yep. Feeding both boys at the same time is a messy, challenging experience."

"You can't fool me—" because she needed something to do with her hands, she got up and retrieved her wine "—you enjoyed every minute of it."

Now, he smiled. "I did." But the smile soon faded. And Kelly knew why.

"You're worried about tomorrow night," she told him.

"You, too."

She nodded. "Hard not to worry when the stakes are this high."

He didn't agree. Instead, Nick motioned toward the door. "I asked the cook to serve our dinner in my office in about an hour. I hope you don't mind."

"I don't. There are fewer windows in your office than the dining room." And that was no doubt the reason he'd arranged it that way. Ditto for insisting that all the drapes be closed and that everyone stay away from the windows and exterior doors.

"Esther heard you mention that you love lasagna," Nick continued. "So she's making that and another of your favorites—key lime pie."

Oh, no. Kelly hoped this wasn't going where she thought it might be going. "My favorite wine. A heavenly bath. Lasagna and key lime pie. Suddenly, I don't like the sound of all of it. Is this your way of saying this is our last night together?"

"No. I just wanted to do something special for you."

She wanted to believe him. Did she ever. But she couldn't. Nick was obviously preparing for the worst.

But she immediately revised that thought when he walked toward her. He didn't pause. He didn't say anything. He simply reached out, put her wineglass aside, hooked his arm around her waist and dragged her to him. Just like that, she was against him.

And then he kissed her.

The kiss came so quickly that it took her a moment to register his intentions. This wasn't a kiss of comfort. Not a last kiss, either. It was a kiss that was meant to lead to one thing and one thing only.

Sex.

Kelly didn't resist. Because after several seconds of Nick's clever kissing, she was surprised she hadn't thought of this sooner.

She wanted him. He obviously wanted her. Their sons were sound asleep in the nursery. And even though there was danger somewhere waiting for them, the danger wasn't here inside the bathroom with them. For a few precious moments, Nick and she could be together.

Even if they shouldn't be.

But Kelly refused to think of that now. Heck, she refused to think about anything except the kiss.

Of course, Nick didn't let it stay just a kiss. He deepened it, fast. Perhaps because he was responding to the urgency already building inside him.

Nick slipped his hand inside her bathrobe and cupped her breast. He broke the kiss only long enough so that he could wet his fingers in his mouth. Then he slid those slippery-wet fingers over her left nipple.

Kelly lost her breath.

"If you're going to stop, this is your chance to do it now," Nick mumbled, a split second before he kissed her neck.

"We're not stopping."

That was obviously Nick's green light because he pushed her robe from her shoulders. It fell to the floor, and they soon followed it.

She was naked.

Nick wasn't.

Kelly fumbled with buttons and his zipper, and then she fumbled again with his boxer briefs. It didn't help that he continued to kiss her during the maddeningly long process. Those kisses not only fueled the flames, they nearly pushed her over the edge.

Once she had him naked and on top of her, it was Nick's turn to fumble. He had to stop the kisses while he retrieved the condom and put it on. Each second seemed like an eternity.

She watched his face as he entered her, though it was next to impossible to see because her vision blurred. Still, Kelly forced herself to focus. She wanted to see him. To remember every last detail.

In case…

But soon cataloging memories was no longer possible. With each deep stroke inside her, the tension built, and her body pinpointed on only one thing.

Nick.

With each stroke her pulse pounded. Her breath raced. She was on fire. And there was no way this kind of fire could last long. So when she could take no more, she slid her arms around him and pulled him close.

And surrendered.

Nick whispered something. Her name, she realized.

With a deep masculine sound rumbling in his throat, he buried his face against her neck and let her take him over the edge.

Moments later they lay there, trying to catch their breaths. And Kelly let the dreamy feel of pleasure slip over her. Her body was sated.

Her mind, however, wasn't.

She had no plans to regret making love with Nick. But she should probably offer him another out. After all, this was no different than it had been in the panic room closet.

But it felt different.

It felt like more. Much, much more. Like something that scared the daylights out of her.

Heaven forbid—it felt like love.

NICK FORCED HIMSELF to get up from the bathroom floor. He scooped a naked Kelly into his arms and took her to her bed.

Where he should have taken her *before* they had sex.

When he walked into her bathroom and saw her standing there, he knew that nothing would stop him from hauling her off to bed. Unfortunately, he hadn't even made it that far. First, a closet wall. Now, the bathroom floor. He had no idea why he couldn't resist Kelly long enough to give her some foreplay and a comfortable mattress.

His body encouraged him to try again just so he could get it right.

But now wasn't the time for more sex. It was the time for him to get some things straight mentally.

"Are you okay?" she whispered.

He glanced at her, tried to smile, but when that failed he kissed her instead. It worked. She made a wistful sigh and snuggled against him. They lay there, basking in the afterglow of great sex.

While he thought about how he could keep Kelly alive.

With Paula and Todd banned from the ranch, he felt marginally safer. He would also instruct his new security crew to keep an eye out for Denny and Cooper. While he was at it, he'd add Rosalinda McMillan's name to his ever-growing list. He didn't want those five people anywhere near Kelly and their sons.

Of course, that left him with a huge problem.

He would have new agents who would be undercover throughout the ranch. And he'd have a new security staff. In other words, he wasn't sure he could trust them any more than he could trust the others. Simply put, anyone could be guilty of trying to kill them. And that still left Eric. Even though Nick had as good as dismissed his brother as being the actual shooter, that wasn't a good approach to take.

Because Eric might be the sole person responsible.

There might be only one hired gun and a greedy, ruthless man who wanted to protect his inheritance by killing the competition.

"You're thinking too hard," she commented.

No way. That was impossible in this situation, and he needed to consider it from all angles.

"If something goes wrong tomorrow night," Nick responded. "There's a suitcase in the closet in the panic room. In it there's plenty of cash, the access codes to a Swiss bank account, airline tickets and fake passports for Greta, Joseph, William and you."

Snuggling time was obviously over. Kelly turned on her side, propped herself up on her elbow and stared at him. Correction—she *glared* at him.

"Excuse me?" she asked.

She'd heard him all right, but she was obviously objecting to his backup plan. Tough. But Nick wasn't budging. "If something goes wrong, you'll need to leave the country. It wouldn't be safe for you to stay here with Eric around."

"And where exactly is your fake passport and plane ticket?"

Nick chose his words carefully. "I'd join you later. After things settle down."

She stared at him. "Just what are you planning to do at the party?"

"Stop Eric." That was the truth.

Kelly latched on to his face with both hands and turned his head to force eye contact. "Tomorrow night you won't do anything stupid. You won't take any unnecessary chances, will you?"

"No."

"Swear it," she insisted.

"I swear. I won't take any unnecessary chances."

And this time it wasn't a lie. He'd take chances all right, but they would be necessary. He had to do whatever it took to stop Eric. If things at the party began to fall apart, if it looked as if Eric would be able to just walk about Scot-free, then Nick would have to do something.

It probably wouldn't take much. Eric would already be primed and ready for battle. Nick would be, too. He knew how to push Eric's buttons, and that's exactly what he would do. It would likely escalate to a gunfight, and at the end of it, Nick knew he had to be the winner.

He just had to be.

If not, then he would condemn Kelly to a life of living hell running from Eric.

Nick was prepared to die to make sure that didn't happen.

Chapter Sixteen

Outside, there was a late-autumn thunderstorm rolling in. Or so Nick said. Kelly hadn't actually been able to see the approaching storm for herself, since Greta, the babies and she had been moved to the panic room an hour and a half earlier.

It was only the beginning of the wait.

This was the moment that Kelly had been dreading since she'd first heard mention of the party. There was nothing she could do to stop Nick's plan. Nor was she certain that stopping it would be the right thing. Something had to be done about Eric. Joseph and William had to be safe.

But that didn't make this goodbye to Nick any easier.

He was already dressed in his tux, and she knew that the guests were arriving. Everything was a "go." And that meant Nick had to leave her and head upstairs to the party.

Nick glanced around the panic room as if checking to make sure that all was secure.

He pointed to the stairs and the door that led to the main house. "The two guards will be posted out there. One inside the closet just outside the internal door. The other will be in the hall."

Kelly nodded. "You trust these men?"

"I've checked their backgrounds and references multiple times. I trust them as much as I trust anyone at this point."

She understood that and prayed that these men would do what they'd been hired to do.

Nick crossed the room, gave Greta a reassuring pat on the hand and leaned down and kissed both boys, who were on the carpeted floor playing with the massive selection of toys. In addition to the toys, they had food, water, extra diapers and beds, everything they needed to make it through the night.

"You can use the surveillance monitor to watch what's going on at the party." Nick checked the monitor on the dressing table to make sure it worked. "But I want you to stay put here."

Kelly had expected him to insist on that. In fact, there was little else she could do. There were two guards, yes, but she was still the last line of defense between Eric and the babies.

Nick caught onto her arm and pulled her away from the others. "I don't think you'll need it, but there's a gun in the safe behind the teddy bear picture," he whispered. He took a tiny cell phone from his pocket and pressed it into her hand. "Call me if there's an emergency. The number is already programmed in. If you need me, I'll be here as fast as humanly possible."

She knew he would be. Because she couldn't gather enough breath to speak, Kelly simply nodded again.

"Everything will be okay," Nick assured her, and he sealed it with a kiss.

And that was it. No long, lingering looks. No extended farewells. It was too painful for Nick to do those things. He simply turned, walked up the stairs and disappeared.

Just like that, he was gone, and Kelly immediately thought of a dozen things that she should have said to him. Like "Be careful." Or "Do you have any idea how much you mean to me?" Or the ultimate P.S.— "I'm falling in love with you."

Okay. It was a good thing she hadn't made that particular confession. Nick already had too much on his mind without her adding the emotional stuff.

"You should try to relax," Greta suggested.

That was impossible, but Kelly knew she had to do something or she'd explode. So she laid the phone on the changing table and sank down on the floor next to the babies. Both immediately made their way toward her with Joseph walking and William crawling. They climbed into her lap, and even Kelly's dark mood couldn't stop her from smiling.

She took the opportunity to read them *Green Eggs and Ham*. Well, parts of it anyway. Her sons had very short attention spans so the reading session turned into a play session and then into wrestling match.

The minutes still crawled by.

While she played with the boys, she continued to glance at the clock and the monitor. She saw the guests meander into the great room. She even spotted Nick. But she couldn't find the guest of honor or Eric.

On the screen she could see one of the newly hired guns standing at the back of the room. He was easy to notice because he was the only male in the room who wasn't wearing a tux. He had a black baseball cap slung low over his face. While Kelly watched, she saw the man slide his hand inside his jacket. He took out his gun.

And then the screen went blank.

Greta must have noticed it as well because both of them got to their feet and went to the portable surveillance unit. Kelly pressed the buttons to change the camera angle.

Still blank.

Just a screen filled with fog-gray static.

"You think everything's all right?" Greta asked.

No, she didn't, especially since she'd seen the guard take out his gun. But Kelly kept that info to herself. She grabbed the cell phone that Nick had given her and pressed the button to call the number that he'd programmed in.

More static.

Kelly tried again, and again, frantically stabbing the buttons and praying that the call would connect.

It didn't.

"What's wrong?" Greta asked.

"Someone has jammed the cell phone and the security system. Or maybe it's just some sort of temporary glitch."

Greta put her fingers to her mouth to suppress what would no doubt have been a gasp. Kelly knew she was terrified. My God. What was going on up there? She didn't know, but it couldn't be good.

"Nick could be in danger," Kelly mumbled.

She didn't waste any time. She hurried toward the safe behind the teddy bear picture and retrieved the Glock that Nick had said would be there.

"You can't leave," Greta insisted. "Mr. Lattimer said to stay here."

True. But Kelly couldn't have stayed put even if she'd wanted to. And she didn't want to do that at all. She wanted to check on Nick. Correction: she *had* to check on him. A dozen deadly things could be happening in that great room.

"I'm only going to the top of the stairs to speak to the guard," she explained to Greta. "Maybe he knows what's going on."

With luck, the guard would have a simple explanation and an assurance that all was well.

Greta automatically gathered up the boys, and she took them into the large bathroom that was just off the main area. Kelly waited until the bathroom door was shut before she barreled up the stairs.

When she reached the top, she knocked on the door to alert the guard that she was about to open it. Kelly didn't wait for him to respond, she opened the double set of locks and peered out.

It was pitch-black. All the lights were off, and the guard was there, taking up practically the entire doorway.

"There might be trouble," Kelly informed him. "Something's wrong with the phone line and the surveillance system."

He didn't respond, but she figured he was probably wearing some kind of communicator fitted into his ear. She tapped his shoulder.

He still didn't answer.

But he did move. He fell forward and crumpled into a heap on the floor.

Kelly didn't have time to react. She certainly didn't have time to turn and run back into the panic room so she could lock the door. Someone knocked the Glock from her hand, and she felt the cold hard steel jam against the side of her head.

And Kelly knew she was in serious trouble.

NICK CHECKED HIS WATCH again and cursed under his breath.

Where the hell was his brother?

Everything was in place, including the bait, Marcus Durham, who had just arrived with his fiancée. But there was no sign of Eric. Maybe Eric had decided this was too risky after all.

And if so, all of this had been for nothing.

Outside, there was a storm brewing, and Nick could hear the occasional rumble of thunder. It sounded minor compared to the storm inside his body. This had to be over, soon, because he couldn't put Kelly and their sons through another night of danger.

Nick forced himself to look pleasant and greet his guests, but he tried to keep a vigilant watch on everything going on around him. He noticed the guard in the corner. The man drew his weapon, and that had Nick dropping the pleasant pretense. He slipped his hand in his tux jacket so he could have easy access to his own gun, and he crossed the room and approached the guard.

"Problem?" Nick asked.

"The guards at the gate said there's been some kind of glitch with the exterior surveillance cameras.

They're not working, and it's possible they haven't been fully operational all night."

Nick didn't even try to muffle his profanity. "How did that happen?"

"They're trying to figure that out. There were recorded images being relayed onto the screens so the men didn't think anything was out of the ordinary."

Nick was about to call those men at the front gate, but the guard tipped his head toward the adjacent entry where another guest had made his entrance.

Eric.

His brother, however, didn't come into the great room. He walked right past the butler, another security guard in disguise, turned and headed down the hall.

"Your brother said he's going to the bathroom," the guard relayed through the tiny communicator in Nick's left ear.

"Watch him carefully," Nick insisted.

He took out his cell phone and punched in the numbers to call Kelly just to make sure that everything was okay.

All he heard was static.

Hell.

Nick hurried across the great room so he could go through the back hall to the panic room. He didn't make it far. The housekeeper stepped out from the kitchen and practically ran right into him.

"You have a call, sir," she said.

Praying it was Kelly, he snatched the phone from her. But it wasn't Kelly's voice that greeted him.

"Hello, Nick," the person said. The caller was obviously speaking through a voice scrambler, making it impossible to recognize who was on the other end of the line.

"Where's Kelly?" Nick immediately asked.

"She's safe. For now. She won't be, though, if you don't come to the stables, the one where you have that new palomino quarantined. Come alone. Oh, and Nick, you'd better hurry. Because if you don't, Kelly, the nanny, William and Joseph will be dead within the next three minutes."

KELLY WAS SHIVERING. Cold rain soaked every inch of her jeans and sweater, but she didn't care. She had only one thought on her mind—protect Joseph and William from this ski-mask-wearing kidnapper who'd forced them at gunpoint from the panic room and had "ushered" them to the stables.

Both William and Joseph were crying, but thankfully both had been semisheltered with blankets so they weren't wet and cold. Unlike Greta and her. Greta was shivering, as well, while she tried to comfort William. Kelly tried to do the same for Joseph.

But it was impossible.

The babies could no doubt sense danger. Kelly certainly could. The sounds of the rain and thunder blended with the sound of her own pulse crashing in her ears. She was terrified for the boys, but she couldn't let that immobilize her. She had to do something to keep them all alive.

The kidnapper motioned for them to move to the corner of the stables, right next to a stall with an enormous palomino. A horse she'd heard Nick say was in "quarantine" because it had some aggressive behavior and needed to be temporarily separated from the other animals. Kelly hadn't needed anything else to raise her adrenaline level, but that did it.

So did the call that the kidnapper made.

The kidnapper wore some kind of device around his or her throat, and that device made it impossible to identify the person speaking. The person told Nick to come to the stables or they'd all die within three minutes.

Kelly wouldn't let that happen.

But now, unfortunately, Nick was walking straight into the line of fire. Because this person likely would try to kill them as soon as Nick arrived. And that wasn't all.

There was a gas can and a lighter in the center of the stable floor.

This person probably intended to burn down the place so there wouldn't be any incriminating evidence left behind.

Kelly gave Joseph what she hoped was a reassuring kiss and pat on the back, but she didn't take her attention off the kidnapper. In addition to the ski mask and voice device, the person wore a bulky parka, making it impossible to tell if this was a man or woman. He or she was average height—probably around five-ten. But other than Cooper, that description fit any and all of their suspects.

Including Eric.

God, was it possible that he was behind that mask?

Or was this someone on his payroll. Todd Burgess, maybe? Or Paula Barker? Of course, it could also be Rosalinda McMillan, Eric's former secretary. Or, heaven forbid, even Denny. It sickened her that she couldn't rule him out.

Greta sank down on the hay-strewn floor and moved Joseph to her side so she could try to shield him from the gun that their kidnapper had aimed at them. Kelly did the same, but she crouched down instead of sitting so she could launch herself at their attacker if it became necessary.

"Why are you doing this?" Kelly asked.

The person didn't answer, shifting attention between them and the stable door.

Where Nick would come through any second.

Kelly figured the kidnapper would try to shoot Nick first and then would turn that gun on them. Since Kelly couldn't let that happen, she eased Joseph closer to Greta so that the nanny could hold on to both boys. Then, Kelly frantically looked around for anything she could use as a weapon. There was nothing.

Except the stable gate.

Kelly was right next to the lever that would open the gate. It wasn't much protection, since a bullet could easily go through the openings in the metal. Plus, there was the horse. If she opened the gate, it might bolt and do heaven knew what. Still, it was a risk she had to take to save the babies and Nick.

Even over the sounds of the storm, Kelly heard footsteps. Someone was running. Nick, probably. That garnered the kidnapper's attention, and Kelly used that opportunity to slide her hand over the gate lever.

She didn't open the gate. Not yet. But she crouched there with her heart pounding and her breath racing out of control. Waiting for the right moment.

But the right moment didn't come.

The kidnapper stormed toward her, moving just behind Kelly to use her as a human shield. Sweet heaven. Nick wouldn't come in with guns blazing, but a shootout seemed inevitable.

The stable doors flew open, and Kelly braced herself to see Nick and to hear the shot that would almost certainly be fired at him.

"Watch out!" Kelly yelled.

But the warning wasn't necessary. Because there was no one in the stable doorway.

That obviously didn't please the kidnapper, who cursed viciously, hooked an arm around Kelly's neck and repositioned her so that she was in the line of fire. The only advantage that Kelly had was that she was able to keep her hand on the gate latch.

"Show yourself or I'll kill her now," the kidnapper called out.

Kelly's breath stalled in her throat, and she waited, bracing herself for whatever was about to happen.

Nick appeared in the doorway with his hands on his head. A show of surrender. And if he had a gun, it wasn't visible.

"Let Kelly go," Nick insisted.

"Get inside," the kidnapper answered. "Close the doors."

Nick did as ordered, and the moment the doors were shut, the kidnapper moved away from Kelly and aimed the gun at Nick. Even though the light was dim in the stables, Kelly had no trouble seeing the gloved hand of the kidnapper tense around the gun.

And the trigger.

That was Kelly's cue. She couldn't wait. She pulled back the gate lever, and the metallic creaking sound that it made seemed to echo through the entire stables.

That sound alerted the kidnapper, who whirled around, re-aiming the gun at Kelly.

Then all hell broke loose.

Nick launched himself at the kidnapper. Kelly dove

to the side. Away from Greta and the babies so that she could hopefully draw any gunfire away from them.

She heard Nick yell for her to get down. Kelly yelled for him to do the same. That didn't stop the kidnapper from coming after her—or the massive palomino from bolting from the stall.

The horse blocked Nick from getting to her.

Knowing she would die if she didn't do something, Kelly took a huge risk. Instead of moving away from the kidnapper, she turned and barreled right toward the gun that was aimed at her chest. Obviously, the kidnapper hadn't expected her to do that, because there was just a moment of hesitation. A split second of time. But that was all the time Kelly needed to ram into the kidnapper.

Both fell to the stable floor.

Around them were the sounds of chaos: deafening thunder, babies crying, the horse rearing and snorting, and Nick shouting. Kelly wanted Greta to get herself and the babies out of there, but the woman was trapped because of the horse. Maneuvering past it would be too dangerous.

Kelly fought, going for the kidnapper's gun. It was their best chance at survival. But she heard the loud thud behind her. Looked up. And saw that the horse's front hooves were about to come down right on her.

She rolled to the side. So did the kidnapper. Just as Nick managed to get around the rearing horse.

The kidnapper turned the gun on Nick.

Kelly reached out, latching on to whatever she could. She caught onto the stretchy ski mask, ripping it off the kidnapper.

And came face-to-face with the person who obviously wanted them dead.

Chapter Seventeen

Nick kept his attention on the kidnapper's gun. Not on Kelly. Not on the babies' now-frantic sobs. Not on the mare that was totally out of control and would likely hurt herself and the rest of them.

His focus was only on the gun.

He had to get it away from the kidnapper before Kelly was shot.

Nick ducked around the mare and raced toward Kelly. She was on the ground in a wrestling match with the kidnapper. It was a battle she was on the verge of losing. Her opponent was larger and much stronger.

When Nick made it to them, the kidnapper spun around, and the light from the overhead dangling bulb illuminated the person's face.

It was Paula Barker.

His gaze met hers, and in her eyes he could see not anger or venom but her determination not to lose this battle. She cursed, caught Kelly by her hair and got them both to their feet.

Paula also put the gun to Kelly's head.

Kelly's eyes were filled with determination, too, and Nick knew that in an all-out battle, Kelly would find a way to win. They both would. Because their children's lives were at stake.

"Stay where you are," Paula ordered him.

Nick froze—for the time being—and he tried to figure out what to do. This situation was already out of hand. But it could easily turn deadly if he didn't handle this the right way.

"You're on Eric's payroll," Nick said, hoping to distract Paula.

The attempt at distraction didn't work. With Kelly in tow, Paula began to back up toward Greta and the babies.

Nick tried again. "You jammed the security equipment and the cell phones. You don't want Eric brought to justice because he's your real boss."

Again Paula had no reaction other than to yell out, "Keep your hands in the air where I can see them."

He did. Though he wouldn't hold that particular stance for long. He had his gun tucked into his slide holster in the back waist of his pants, and he was definitely going to retrieve it so he could stop this woman.

Paula volleyed glances between Nick and Greta. Probably because she thought that Greta might try something. Nick was almost positive that she wouldn't. Or rather, she *couldn't*. Greta was in her own struggle to hang on to both boys, who were crying and squirming to get away from her.

"You know this is a mistake," Nick said to Paula. "Eric's paying you to do his dirty work, but in the end you'll be caught. You'll go to jail. And he'll walk away scot-free." He kept his voice calm and began to inch down his hands so he could go for his gun.

He might as well have been talking to himself because Paula didn't even acknowledge that he'd spoken. She was focused totally on the task, and it didn't take him long to figure out what exactly that was.

Paula made her way toward the gasoline. And she was careful about it, too. She kept herself between Kelly and the babies. Even if Nick could manage to draw his gun, he wouldn't be able to fire unless Paula moved out of position. He had to think of something fast to get her to do that.

Without taking her attention off him, Paula used her foot to knock over the metal can. The liquid spilled onto the hay-littered floor.

She was going to set the place on fire.

Kelly's eyes widened, and she shook her head. Nick knew they couldn't wait any longer. He dropped his arms and reached for his gun. In the same exact moment, Kelly dropped her weight and sank below Paula.

Paula aimed at Kelly and was no doubt about to fire.

"No!" Nick yelled. He drew his gun.

It worked.

A little too well.

Paula took aim at him. Nick dove to the side just as she pulled the trigger.

THE SOUND OF THE SHOT tore through the stables.

It was deafening. And it caused the babies to shriek even louder and the horse to rear in a mad panic.

Kelly pushed all the noise and the horrific sounds aside so she could check and see if Nick was okay.

He seemed to move in slow motion. Or maybe that was the way her brain was trying to process all of this pandemonium. Nick scrambled toward an empty stall and dove inside it just in time.

Paula's bullet sliced away a chunk of a wooden post that was close to where Nick had been standing. Too close. If he hadn't moved when he did, he would have been dead.

Kelly watched in horror as Paula aimed again at Nick. She couldn't risk another shot being fired at him, so Kelly rammed her body into Paula's back.

Both of them tumbled forward.

Nick shouted something that Kelly couldn't hear with all the surrounding noise. And she didn't take the time to try to understand what he'd said. Kelly grabbed Paula's right wrist and dug her nails into the woman's flesh.

Paula didn't just give up. She fought like a crazed demon. And that was probably because the stakes were astronomical for her.

But not as high as they were for Kelly and Nick. So Kelly continued to hold Paula's wrist until the woman elbowed Kelly in the jaw. The impact sent Kelly flying back, but she immediately scrambled forward so she could grab Paula's shooting hand again. She needed to get that gun away from Paula.

Kelly soon had help. She heard footsteps a split second before Nick reached down into the scuffle and yanked Paula out by the hair, wrenched the gun from her hand and kicked it away. It landed in the area where the horse was pawing.

But Paula wasn't ready to surrender.

The woman obviously had plenty of defense training because she aimed her fist at Nick's jaw. He ducked. Paula came at him again. Nick shifted his position, stepping slightly to the side, and when Paula launched herself at him, he put her in a headlock and dropped to the ground. Paula's head hit the concrete floor, the sound thudding over the other noise.

Paula went limp.

Nick immediately checked for a pulse. "She's alive," he relayed to Kelly. His breath was gusting and his chest pumped as if starved for air. "Are you okay?"

She nodded and glanced at the boys. Though they were both crying at the tops of their lungs, they seemed physically unharmed. However, Kelly didn't want to think of the trauma this had caused.

Nick made it to her and pulled her into his arms for what had to be the shortest reassurance hug ever. Still, it was heaven. Nick and the babies were unharmed.

"We're getting out of here *now*," Nick insisted. "I'll phone the police from the car. They can come out and arrest Paula."

He didn't have to tell Kelly twice. She sprang from the floor. So did Greta, and Kelly hurried to her so that she could take one of the boys.

Nick dodged the rearing horse again and raced to the front of the stables. "Stay put until I make sure everything is clear."

But the words had hardly left his mouth when the stable doors burst open.

A truck rammed through the steel and the wood, and the impact threw Nick back. He went sprawling to the floor. So did his weapon.

Eric stepped from the vehicle. A gun in each hand. And the first thing he did was fire at the gun that Nick was frantically trying to reach. The shot caused Nick's weapon to skitter across the floor away from him.

"Don't go for it," Eric warned through clenched teeth.

He was drenched, rain dripping from his hair

and face. And he was obviously pissed off. He got even angrier when he glanced at an unconscious Paula on the floor.

"Stupid bitch," he mumbled.

Eric fired nasty glances at all five of them in the stables. "You all should have been dead by now, and the place should have been on fire so that your bald-headed security honcho could be set up to take the blame. That's the last time I hire a woman to do a man's job."

He aimed a gun at Kelly but divided his attention between Nick and her.

Eric went toward the gas can that was lying on its side. But that wasn't all he did. He aimed the gun in his left hand at Greta who was cradling Joseph in her arms.

"You two first," Eric announced. "Don't worry. The rest won't be far behind."

Fear and anger raged through Kelly. She was sick and tired of this monster trying to destroy her family. She didn't think, didn't hesitate. She pushed William at Greta. She heard a feral sound vibrate in her throat, and she ran at Eric, putting herself between his gun and Joseph.

That didn't stop Eric. He fired just as Nick tackled him from behind.

Kelly didn't wait to see if she'd been hit. She charged toward Nick and Eric, who were in a fight for the guns that Eric still had in his hands.

The horse stopped her.

The palomino moved between the scuffle and her. For just a moment, she lost sight of Nick, and it caused her to lose her breath. God, he had to be all right.

Kelly picked up the empty gas can, intending to use it to bash Eric. She moved around the side of the stable, trying to avoid the horse. It wasn't easy to do. The animal seemed to charge right at her, and the old fears returned. It didn't matter, however. No phobia was going to stop her from getting to Nick.

The horse was so close to her that she felt its hot breath snort against her face. Still, Kelly worked her way around the stalls and spotted Nick.

He was on the floor with Eric. Nick had hold of both of Eric's wrists. The death grip prevented Eric from aiming the guns, but it didn't stop him.

Eric's right index finger was on the trigger.

And Kelly watched in horror as he pulled it.

There was another thick blast, and Kelly saw the impact. Wood and splinters spewed from the back of the stable wall.

"Try to get the boys out," Kelly shouted to Greta. Though she wasn't sure Greta could manage to get past the horse.

Kelly started toward Eric and Nick again. But she didn't make it to them in time. Nick slammed his brother's hand onto the floor, next to Eric's head.

Just as Eric pulled the trigger again.

Kelly dropped the gas can and rushed to Nick. Greta stopped, too. But it wasn't Nick who'd been hurt. It was Eric. The shot he'd fired had entered his own right temple. There was no need to check for a pulse or any other sign of life.

Eric was dead.

Kelly's breath broke. She felt on the verge of breaking, as well. Her legs gave way, and she would have fallen if Nick hadn't caught her. He hooked his arm around her waist and pulled her to him.

The emotions came at her nonstop. Eric was dead. As horrible as the gruesome sight was in front of her, she couldn't feel grief that he was no longer a threat in their lives.

"It's over," Kelly heard herself say. And she leaned against Nick and let him support her. "It's really over."

"Not quite," someone said.

It was Paula.

Nick and Kelly whirled around, and just on the other side of the palomino, Kelly saw something that turned her blood to ice.

Paula was no longer unconscious. There was a fresh trail of blood seeping from her forehead and onto her parka, but other than that, she seemed alive and well.

She was also armed.

She'd obviously retrieved her gun while Eric and Nick had been fighting.

"Eric is dead," Nick shouted to her. "This is over."

"No. It's not over." Paula was standing several yards in front of Greta and the babies.

And the agent had a lit match in her hand.

She tossed the match onto the gasoline. The blaze was instant.

But Paula merely stepped to one side, took aim and fired at Kelly and Nick.

NICK DIDN'T HAVE TIME to retrieve one of Eric's guns. He caught Kelly and dragged her to the floor with him. The bullet whipped right over his head. But it wasn't a solo shot. Paula fired again and again.

This was Nick's worst nightmare come true. Kelly and the babies were in danger, and even though Eric was out of the picture, Nick might not be able to save them.

The orange flames began to eat their way through the stables, and Nick knew that Greta was trapped. There was no exit in that corner, and she'd have to get past Paula to escape. An impossible task, especially with two babies in tow.

The horse reared again, and Nick used that opportunity to grab Kelly and move her just inside one of the stalls. He didn't pick that one randomly; it was next to the fire extinguisher, which he tore from the wall.

He didn't wait to come up with a plan. There wasn't time for that. He had to react now. Using the mare for cover, he maneuvered himself to the back of the stable. The smoke was already so thick that Paula was coughing and trying to make her way to the front exit.

Nick didn't want to let her escape, but he had to save Greta, Kelly and the babies. Kelly obviously had the same idea, because she raced toward Greta and scooped up the babies in her arms.

Now Nick had to create an escape path for them all.

Unfortunately, Paula was on the other side of the mare and closer to the fresh air. She turned and fired.

Nick jumped in front of Kelly to shield her and then tossed the fire extinguisher to Greta. Putting out that fire was their only chance right now.

He heard Greta spraying the flames, and he raced toward Paula—who was taking aim at Kelly and the boys.

Nick dove toward his brother's body and slid across the floor so that he could snatch up one of the Glocks. He lifted the gun just as Paula whirled toward him and prepared to shoot him.

But Nick fired first.

Paula froze as if in shock. Her startled gaze met his for just a second before she collapsed into a dead heap on the stable floor.

"Kelly?" Nick shouted.

He didn't bother to confirm that Paula was dead because the extinguisher hadn't yet taken care of the flames. The fire was out of control and quickly making its way through the stables.

Nick got to Kelly, who was trying to stomp out the flames, and he latched on to both Greta and her. It was a race for their lives. Thankfully, the mare realized that and bolted out of the opening that Eric had created when he'd crashed through the stable doors with the truck.

Nick wasn't far behind. He grabbed the babies from Kelly, and they ran toward the opening. He felt the heat from the flames and felt his throat close from the smothering smoke. But he didn't stop.

He tightened his grip on the boys and got them all outside into the cold, fresh rain.

Despite the fact that the babies were crying and that they'd just endured a nightmare, they had survived. They were all alive.

But there was no time to celebrate.

Kelly collapsed on the ground in front of him.

Chapter Eighteen

The first thing Kelly saw when she opened her eyes was Nick.

His forehead was bunched up, his eyes beyond intense, and his hair looked as if he'd been shoving his hands through it.

She sat up. Or rather she tried to, but Nick eased her right back down. That's when she realized she was lying on a quilt on the kitchen floor.

"You fainted," Nick explained.

Yes. She remembered that. While she'd been trying to escape, the smoke had gotten to her. But how had she gotten from the stables to the kitchen? It was a good guess that Nick had carried her there.

"Where are the babies?" she managed to ask.

"They're fine." He leaned a little to the side, and she spotted both Joseph and William. Greta was sitting on the floor and was changing them into dry clothes. However, the moment the boys noticed that

Kelly was looking at them, they wiggled out of their nanny's embrace and walked toward Kelly and Nick.

The boys were a welcome sight, even though William was shirtless and Joseph's feet were bare.

Kelly made another attempt to sit up, and this time Nick didn't stop her.

"Mama's going to be all right," Nick assured the boys.

William and Joseph picked up on the sounds, and both said the words that were absolutely precious to Kelly. "Ma-ma."

Even after everything that'd happened, that made her smile.

Nick reached over and pressed the intercom that was on the counter next to her. "Zeke, let me know when the ambulance gets here."

"I will," Zeke answered. "Oh, and Cooper's here. He'll deal with the sheriff and anything else that comes up."

"Ambulance?" Kelly repeated. Her smile vanished, and she glanced at the boys, Nick and her own body. Other than some minor scrapes and bruises on her hands, they were all fine.

"The ambulance is a precaution," Nick added softly, obviously trying not to alarm her.

Kelly eased away from the babies, who were now more interested in exploring the antique-glass cabinet knobs, and she took Nick's sleeve.

"What's wrong?" she asked. And her imagination leaped to the worst possible conclusion. "Eric and Paula aren't really dead and they got away."

"No. They're both really dead." He shook his head, groaned and rubbed his hand over his face. "But I nearly got you killed—again."

Oh. So, that's what his dour look was about. Kelly was actually relieved. What they'd been through was horrible, and witnessing two violent deaths hadn't been easy. But considering what could have happened, they were lucky.

Kelly moved closer to Nick and because they both needed it she kissed him. He didn't exactly return the kiss, though. Instead he pulled her into his arms and gave her a very hard hug.

"There's no reason to feel guilty," Kelly whispered.

Nick didn't answer. And that's when she knew she had to do something—even if they weren't alone in the room.

"I'm not giving you an out this time," she said, putting her mouth right against his ear. "It was never just sex to me."

He pulled back and met her gaze. "It wasn't for me, either."

Kelly's smile returned. That was far more than she could have hoped for. "Good. Maybe we can build on what we've already started."

"No."

Kelly shook her head, certain that she'd misunderstood him. "No?"

"No maybes. I'm going straight for the bottom line here. Will you marry me?"

She thought she might faint again. The blood rushed to her head. Her throat tightened. She couldn't speak.

William draped a pot holder over her head, giggled and gave her a sloppy kiss on the cheek. Not to be outdone, Joseph kissed her, too.

Kelly was still sitting there, dumbfounded and with a potholder on her head, when the housekeeper came rushing in. "Here it is, sir. I took it from the vault." She handed Nick a small velvet pouch.

Nick glanced inside, thanked the woman and then promptly gathered Joseph and William into the crooks of each of his arms. "Will you marry me?" Nick repeated. "We can raise our children together."

Kelly had every intention of saying yes, but Nick apparently wasn't finished. He had William and Joseph each catch one side of the string on the pouch, and he prompted them to hand it to her.

She took it and extracted the ring. It was a simply set yellow diamond. And perfect. It was exactly the kind of ring she would have chosen.

"It belonged to my grandmother," Nick explained. "Now say yes."

Because she wanted this moment to be perfect, she raked the potholder from her head, moved closer so she could gather Nick and her sons into her arms.

"Say yes," someone shouted.

It took her a moment to realize it was Zeke. And his voice was coming from over the intercom.

"How many people heard this proposal?" Nick asked.

"Everybody in the house," was Zeke's response.

Kelly winced. So much for making this a perfect moment. But even with Nick's very public proposal, it was still perfect.

Nick nodded. "Good. I'm glad everyone heard. If she says yes, it'll save us from having to make an announcement."

All eyes turned toward her. Nick. Greta. And even the boys, who seemed to sense that something huge and wonderful was about to happen.

Kelly kissed William and Joseph on their cheeks and saved an adult kiss for Nick. Considering they were in an embrace with two active squirming boys, the kiss was still hot and memorable.

Just like her husband-to-be.

"Yes," Kelly answered. "I'll marry you. And, yes, we'll raise our sons together."

And she'd never been more certain of anything in her life.

* * * * *

*Be sure to look for another
Five-Alarm Babies Story
by Delores Fossen later in 2007!*

Welcome to cowboy country...

Turn the page for a sneak preview of
TEXAS BABY
by
Kathleen O'Brien
An exciting new title from
Harlequin Superromance for everyone
who loves stories about the West.

Harlequin Superromance—
Where life and love weave together in emotional
and unforgettable ways.

CHAPTER ONE

CHASE TRANSFERRED his gaze to the road and identified a foreign spot on the horizon. A car. Almost half a mile away, where the straight, tree-lined drive met the public road. He could tell it was coming too fast, but judging the speed of a vehicle moving straight toward you was tricky.

It wasn't until it was about two hundred yards away that he realized the driver must be drunk...or crazy. Or both.

The guy was going maybe sixty. On a private drive, out here in ranch country, where kids or horses or tractors or stupid chickens might come darting out any minute, that was criminal. Chase straightened from his comfortable slouch and waved his hands.

"Slow down, you fool," he called out. He took the porch steps quickly and began walking fast down the driveway.

The car veered oddly, from one lane to another,

then up onto the slight rise of the thick green spring grass. It just barely missed the fence.

"Slow down, damn it!"

He couldn't see the driver, and he didn't recognize this automobile. It was small and old, and couldn't have cost much even when it was new. It was probably white, but now it needed either a wash or a new paint job or both.

"Damn it, what's wrong with you?"

At the last minute, he had to jump away, because the idiot behind the wheel clearly wasn't going to turn to avoid a collision. He couldn't believe it. The car kept coming, finally slowing a little, but it was too late.

Still going about thirty miles an hour, it slammed into the large, white-brick pillar that marked the front boundaries of the house. The pillar wasn't going to give an inch, so the car had to. The front end folded up like a paper fan.

It seemed to take forever for the car to settle, as if the trauma happened in slow motion, reverberating from the front to the back of the car in ripples of destruction. The front windshield suddenly seemed to ice over with lethal bits of glassy frost. Then the side windows exploded.

The front driver's door wrenched open, as if the car wanted to expel its contents. Metal buckled hideously. Small pieces, like hubcaps and mirrors, skipped and ricocheted insanely across the oyster-shell driveway.

Finally, everything was still. Into the silence, a plume of steam shot up like a geyser, smelling of rust and heat. Its snake-like hiss almost smothered the low, agonized moan of the driver.

Chase's anger had disappeared. He didn't feel anything but a dull sense of disbelief. Things like this didn't happen in real life. Not in his life. Maybe the sun had actually put him to sleep....

But he was already kneeling beside the car. The driver was a woman. The frosty glass-ice of the windshield was dotted with small flecks of blood. She must have hit it with her head, because just below her hairline a red liquid was seeping out. He touched it. He tried to wipe it away before it reached her eyebrow, though, of course that made no sense at all. Her eyes were shut.

Was she conscious? Did he dare move her? Her dress was covered in glass, and the metal of the car was sticking out lethally in all the wrong places.

Then he remembered, with an intense relief, that every good medical man in the county was here, just behind the house, drinking his champagne. He found his phone and paged Trent.

The woman moaned again.

Alive, then. Thank God for that.

He saw Trent coming toward him, starting out at a lope, but quickly switching to a full run.

"Get Dr. Marchant," Chase called. "Don't bother with 911."

Trent didn't take long to assess the situation. A fraction of a second, and he began pulling out his cell phone and running toward the house.

The yelling seemed to have roused the woman. She opened her eyes. They were blue and clouded with pain and confusion.

"Chase," she said.

His breath stalled. His head pulled back. "What?"

Her only answer was another moan, and he wondered if he had imagined the word. He reached around her and put his arm behind her shoulders. She was tiny. Probably petite by nature, but surely way too thin. He could feel her shoulder blades pushing against her skin, as fragile as the wishbone in a turkey.

She seemed to have passed out, so he put his other arm under her knees and lifted her out. He tried to avoid the jagged metal, but her skirt caught on a piece and the tearing sound seemed to wake her again.

"No," she said. "Please."

"I'm just trying to help," he said. "It's going to be all right."

She seemed profoundly distressed. She wriggled in his arms, and she was so weak, like a broken bird. It made him feel too big and brutish. And intrusive. As if touching her this way, his bare hands against the warm skin behind her knees, were somehow a transgression.

He wished he could be more delicate. But he smelled gasoline, and he knew it wasn't safe to leave her here.

Finally he heard the sound of voices, as guests began to run around the side of the house, alerted by Trent. Dr. Marchant was at the front, racing toward them as if he were forty instead of seventy. Susannah was right behind him, her green dress floating around her trim legs.

"Please," the woman in his arms murmured again. She looked at him, the expression in her blue eyes lost and bewildered. He wondered if she might be on drugs. Hitting her head on the windshield might account for this unfocused, glazed look, but it couldn't explain the crazy driving.

"Please, put me down. Susannah... The wedding..."

Chase's arms tightened instinctively, and he froze in his tracks. She whimpered, and he realized he might be hurting her. "Say that again?"

"The wedding. I have to stop it."

* * * * *

Be sure to look for TEXAS BABY,
available September 11, 2007,
as well as other fantastic Superromance titles
available in September.

Welcome to Cowboy Country...

TEXAS BABY

by *Kathleen O'Brien*

#1441

Chase Clayton doesn't know what to think.
A beautiful stranger has just crashed his
engagement party, demanding that he not
marry because she's pregnant with his baby.
But the kicker is—he's never seen her before.

Look for TEXAS BABY and other fantastic
Superromance titles on sale September 2007.

Available wherever books are sold.

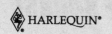
HARLEQUIN®

EVERLASTING LOVE™

Every great love has a story to tell™

Third time's a charm.

Texas summers. Charlie Morrison.
Jasmine Boudreaux has always connected
the two. Her relationship with Charlie
begins and ends in high school. Twenty
years later it begins again—and ends again.
Now fate has stepped in one more time—
will Jazzy and Charlie finally give in to
the love they've shared all this time?

Look for

Summer After Summer
by
Ann DeFee

Available September
wherever books are sold.

www.eHarlequin.com

HESAS0907

REQUEST YOUR FREE BOOKS!

2 FREE NOVELS PLUS 2 FREE GIFTS!

HARLEQUIN®

INTRIGUE®

Breathtaking Romantic Suspense

YES! Please send me 2 FREE Harlequin Intrigue® novels and my 2 FREE gifts. After receiving them, if I don't wish to receive any more books, I can return the shipping statement marked "cancel." If I don't cancel, I will receive 6 brand-new novels every month and be billed just $4.24 per book in the U.S., or $4.99 per book in Canada, plus 25¢ shipping and handling per book and applicable taxes, if any*. That's a savings of close to 15% off the cover price! I understand that accepting the 2 free books and gifts places me under no obligation to buy anything. I can always return a shipment and cancel at any time. Even if I never buy another book from Harlequin, the two free books and gifts are mine to keep forever.

182 HDN EEZ7 382 HDN EEZK

Name	(PLEASE PRINT)	
Address		Apt. #
City	State/Prov.	Zip/Postal Code

Signature (if under 18, a parent or guardian must sign)

Mail to the **Harlequin Reader Service®**:
IN U.S.A.: P.O. Box 1867, Buffalo, NY 14240-1867
IN CANADA: P.O. Box 609, Fort Erie, Ontario L2A 5X3

Not valid to current Harlequin Intrigue subscribers.

Want to try two free books from another line?
Call 1-800-873-8635 or visit www.morefreebooks.com.

* Terms and prices subject to change without notice. NY residents add applicable sales tax. Canadian residents will be charged applicable provincial taxes and GST. This offer is limited to one order per household. All orders subject to approval. Credit or debit balances in a customer's account(s) may be offset by any other outstanding balance owed by or to the customer. Please allow 4 to 6 weeks for delivery.

Your Privacy: Harlequin is committed to protecting your privacy. Our Privacy Policy is available online at www.eHarlequin.com or upon request from the Reader Service. From time to time we make our lists of customers available to reputable firms who may have a product or service of interest to you. If you would prefer we not share your name and address, please check here. ☐

HI07

HARLEQUIN®

Mediterranean NIGHTS™

Experience glamour, elegance, mystery and revenge aboard the high seas....

Coming in September 2007...

BREAKING ALL THE RULES

by

Marisa Carroll

Aboard the cruise ship *Alexandra's Dream* for some R & R, sports journalist Lola Sandler is surprised to spot pro-golfer Eric Lashman. Years after walking away from the pro circuit with no explanation to the public, Eric now finds himself teaching aboard a cruise ship.

Lola smells a career-making exposé... but their developing relationship may force her to make a difficult choice.

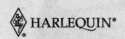

HARLEQUIN®

INTRIGUE®

COMING NEXT MONTH

#1011 RESTLESS WIND by Aimée Thurlo
Brotherhood of Warriors
Entrusted with the secrets of the Brotherhood of Warriors,
Dana Seles must aid Ranger Blueeyes to prevent the secret Navajo
order from extinction.

#1012 MEET ME AT MIDNIGHT by Jessica Andersen
Lights Out (Book 4 of 4)
On what was to be their first date, Secret Service agent Ty Jones
and Gabriella Solano have only hours to rescue the kidnapped vice
president.

#1013 INTIMATE DETAILS by Dana Marton
Mission: Redemption
On a mission to recover stolen WMDs, Gina Torno is caught by
Cal Spencer. Do they have conflicting orders or is each just playing
hard to get?

#1014 BLOWN AWAY by Elle James
After an American embassy bombing, T. J. Barton thought new love
Sean McNeal died in the explosion. But when he reappears, T.J. and
Sean must shadow the country's most powerful citizens in order to
stop a high-class conspiracy.

#1015 NINE-MONTH PROTECTOR by Julie Miller
The Precinct: Vice Squad
After Sarah Cartwright witnesses a mob murder, it's up to Detective
Cooper Bellamy to protect her—and her unborn child. But has he
crossed the line in falling for his best friend's sister?

#1016 BODYGUARD CONFESSIONS by Donna Young
When the royal palace of Taer is attacked, Quamar Bazan Al Asadi
begins a desperate race across the Sahara with presidential daughter
Anna Cambridge and a five-month-old royal heir. Can they restore
order before the rebels close in?

www.eHarlequin.com